Rider's Game

The American West Series

Laura Stapleton

CONTENTS

ACKNOWLEDGEMENTS

I couldn't have written this without William E. Hill's The Pony Express Trail book. His research helped immensely. Any historical mistakes in Rider's Desire are my own or created for literary license.

CHAPTER ONE

Fiona O'Brien shook her head at the sound of the slamming door. None of the Pony Express riders seemed to know how to shut anything properly. The boys left beds unmade, cards and books scattered all over in the main room, and she'd acquired quite the collection of lost items. Wonderful for her brother, Mason, when she gifted him unclaimed items, but not so good for her. Plus, those "boys" were often grown men.

She tsked-tsked to herself and wiped her flour covered hands on her apron. At least the Carson City station had a wonderful kitchen, one of the best she'd used since leaving Ireland a few years ago. She hummed while putting the biscuits in the oven.

The door banged shut again. The Pony Express riders seemed restless for something to eat, if all that banging was any indication. She couldn't blame them. The beef stew had been cooking all day, and the scent of it left her stomach growling despite a good breakfast. She gathered the bowls, glasses, and silverware before going in and setting the table. As she made everything just so for the riders, she smiled at calling such a rustic room a dining room. Everything was wooden, even the walls and the flooring. She set down the last fork. Certainly, Carson City bore no resemblance to her Irish home; the land wasn't green, the sky not gray, and almost nothing was made of stone.

She paused and stared through the dining room window at the wild landscape outside. The country she now called home endlessly fascinated her. Every time she grew accustomed to the surroundings and missed Ireland, something changed and she fell in love with America all over again.

The wind shifted directions as she watched the trees sway. The building creaked and groaned with the change. Between the dinner smells from the kitchen and perpetually empty stomachs, Fiona knew the current quiet in the station house couldn't last. She hurried to check the biscuits. They were on the doughy side of browning, so she had time to grab a pitcher for their water.

She hurried out back to the water pump. Turning the corner of the building, she ran into a solid wall of a man. "Excuse me," she said and looked up into brown eyes. The color matched his dark hair and the beginnings of a beard. He stood taller than her or even Mason and was a handsome devil of a man. With the same warm red hair and green eyes as hers, her brother was striking, too. The stranger smiled and she couldn't help but grin, too. He had nice teeth, even and white, and enchanting wrinkles in places which showed his good nature.

He grabbed her upper arms to steady her. "Hello

there, miss. Are you sure I have to excuse you? I'd rather keep you here a while for a talk."

She chuckled. "Oh, a charmer, eh?" His good looks gave him an edge. His cheeky smile led her to suspect he knew the effect his grin had on women. She shook her head. "I'd love to, but some of us work for a living." As she pushed past him to the water pump, she added over her shoulder, "And besides, I've no time for talking when there're biscuits in the oven."

"Well then." He put his thumbs in his belt loops and ambled up to her while she drew the water. "I wouldn't want to be the reason why you burned your buns."

She paused in mid-pump and laughed. "No, you wouldn't. My wrath would be the least of your problems." She straightened and walked past him with the full pitcher. "You'd have a half dozen pony boys tanning your hide."

His eyebrows rose and he grinned. "Considering I'm a pony boy, too, I'd like to see them try."

"So would I. If only to see a man full of himself taken down a peg or two," she quipped. His slight chuckle as she went past him to the door proved he took her comment in jest as she'd intended. Him being an Express rider didn't surprise her. He had that lanky build and easy grace of the other pony boys. Add in a scoop of good looks and charm and she found it irresistible to tease him. She held out the water and he took the container. "Make yourself useful and set this on the table. I have biscuits to see to, you know."

"I do, indeed."

She watched him until he left the room before removing the biscuits from the oven. They were a little too brown but the boys wouldn't mind. She dumped them into a bread bowl before setting aside a biscuit for her dinner.

"What else can I do to help?"

Fiona glanced up at him. "I like you. You're my newest friend." Before he could reply with a sassy remark, she gave him a trivet. "I'll need this set on the center of the table." He took it and she picked up the stew pot.

"Why don't I carry the food and you take this," he waved the trivet, "whatever it is?"

"I'm strong enough to carry it myself, thank you." She brushed by him and into the dining room. "Just make sure you do your part."

"Helping a lady is my favorite pastime." He set the trivet down as she'd requested.

She placed the pot on the table and hollered, "Dinner's ready."

"Your biscuits?" he asked.

"In the kitchen, waiting for me to serve them," she replied with a smile. "Have a seat and I'll bring them out." He did as suggested, while pony boys streamed into the room. She grabbed the bread bowl and returned, placing the bowl on the table beside the stew pot. With all the noise of chair legs scraping against the floor and young men talking, she didn't bother saying anything before turning back toward the kitchen.

"You're not eating with us, ma'am?"

She paused, recognizing her new friend's voice, as a chorus of catcalls began. After giving everyone except a frowning Mason her best stern eye, she said, "No, not with you hooligans."

Mason laughed and the others joined in. Even the

handsome stranger smiled before saying, "Come on. Will you, if we promise to be on our best behavior?"

Another round of teasing began. One of the boys filling his bowl said, "Looks like John's sweet on her, fellas. Wonder what Randall is going to say about that."

Fiona glanced at the stranger—John—who sat there with a cat-who-ate-the-cream grin on his face. She put her hands on her hips and stepped forward. "It doesn't matter who likes who. Eat your supper before it's cold and my good cooking is wasted on all of you."

Not giving them a chance to try and change her mind, she turned on her heel and went back into the kitchen. A few of the boys hollered at her, but she ignored them, settling in at the small table to eat her own dinner. As she ate, she noticed the talking in the dining room had returned to the usual level.

She took a bite of stewed vegetables. The flavor was so good, she planned to grow more carrots and potatoes in the small garden next year. The former cook had started a small garden patch and even left a diary of sorts for just the gardening. His last entry had been how the soil and rain hadn't cooperated. She ate a chunk of roast, the meat melting in her mouth. The climate in the States might be hellishly dry compared to home, but the amount of beef available made up for the lack of a daily dose of rain. She closed her eyes and gave a happy hum while chewing.

"I agree. Best supper I've had in a long while."

Fiona opened her eyes with a slight smile and swallowed. "I'd like to take credit but it's due to the ingredients." John held a stack of bowls and Mason followed with glasses and silverware. With both men looking at her and waiting for instructions, she nodded toward the small washtub. "In there, if you please."

John dropped the bowls he carried into a tub she'd set by the door. Mason waited until John finished before leaving the glasses and silverware he'd brought. "She's improved as a cook since we left home, thank God. Else, we'd be crowding out the chickens for their scraps."

Fiona pushed him a bit as he walked by her, embarrassed by the truth. Her first attempts at frying anything had resulted in horribly burned food. Which, Mason never let her forget. She stood and put her dishes in the tub, too, picking up a dishtowel along the way. "Go on, you. It's not as bad as all that."

"Not lately, no." Ducking her attempted slap him with a dishtowel, he grinned and turned to John. Offering his hand, he added, "My name's Mason and this somewhat good cook is my sister, Fiona."

John nodded and shook the other man's hand. "I'd noticed the resemblance." He nodded at Fiona. "Pleased to meet you both. I'm John Williamson."

She smiled and began wiping down the warm stove. "Pleased as well, Mr. Williamson."

"John, please. I'm not much on ceremony and, besides, Mr. Williamson was my father."

Fiona stopped brushing crumbs into her hand. "Was?" she asked and when he nodded, she offered, "I'm sorry to hear that."

"Sorry to say it, too." He shrugged. "Pa died when I was a boy, so it's been just us until lately."

She frowned at the implication and didn't want to ask, but curiosity got the better of her. "Are you on your own, then? Alone in the world?" She caught Mason, standing behind John, as her brother shook his head at her. His silent signal said she was prying too much—and he was right, but still, she couldn't help wanting to know John's story.

"I am alone until I make it to Sacramento." He put his thumbs through his belt loops and leaned against the counter. "Ma took a steamer from Memphis to New Orleans before boarding a larger ship to California."

"Good. I'm glad you have someone who cares for you," she said and echoed his movements in leaning against the counter, too. "It's difficult to be alone in the world." As soon as the words left her mouth, her brother rolled his eyes.

"Yeah." John grinned. "I could have traveled with Ma but wanted the chance to make money. The Pony Express needed help so I signed on. I figured I could see the country and have a little extra in my pocket."

"And maybe meet a few new friends along the way?" she asked. Yes, she was prying into his personal life a bit but a man as handsome as him must have a love pining away for him somewhere. He might talk about freedom, but his words didn't say if he was running toward a woman or away from her. "I don't suppose there's a special someone waiting for you. Unless you truly are a single man and all?"

Mason's open mouthed stare at Fiona almost amused her. He didn't need to be so surprised that she was curious about John, especially since Mason had been curious about the various women they'd seen between here and home. Still, now that her brother's trap was shut and he just frowned at her instead of protesting, she felt like she needed to say, "Not that you have to tell me of course. I'm a stranger and you don't owe me any sort of answer."

He looked at her for a few seconds with a slight smile. "I think you're a lovely lady who's kind hearted enough to fix strange men a good meal. As for being strangers, I'm one to you, too. Your brother back there is wisely hanging around and making sure I don't take liberties with you."

Her eyebrows went up. He might appear casual and unconcerned with his surroundings but John had a keen eye of the people around him. "You might be right," she said. He chuckled and a little tremor of enjoyment went down her spine. Amusing him became her newest favorite thing to do. No ready quips came to mind, of course, because she now wanted to be humorous. She decided on saving the jokes for later and focused on learning more about the new rider. "So what's waiting for you at the end of the Express trail besides your mother? Are you saving money for anything in particular?"

He didn't meet her eyes until after shrugging. "Not really, no. I'm just earning because I can and because card games need a little money to make playing fun."

As she stopped leaning and stood upright, Mason walked up to Fiona. "While you two talk, I have some chores that need doing." He kissed her cheek before giving a nod to John. "A pleasure."

"Same here."

So. The man played card games for money. As she watched him leave, Fiona couldn't help but grin a little. Mason had known that any interest she might have had in John was finished the moment he mentioned gambling. She looked down at the dishcloth still in her hand, folded up into a small square. With enough experience in what gaming did to a person and their family, she didn't want to listen to the man jabber on about playing, losing money, and playing again. "I should start cleaning the kitchen and getting ready for the morning, too."

"Why do I suspect I've said something wrong?"

"From how the conversation is at an end and I'm shooing you from my kitchen?" she asked and he nodded. "I'm not sure you need to know, really." When the skeptical expression remained on his face, she took pity on him. Everyone in their hometown knew the story, so she hadn't needed to tell anyone outright.

She looked at John's puzzled expression. He truly didn't seem to know why the conversation soured. Maybe gambling wasn't the problem here, or for him, as it'd been at home for her and Mason's father. She unfolded and refolded the drying dishcloth in her hands and began, "I suppose a bit of truth won't hurt you. Da gambled away our inheritance money." Now that she had started, the words tumbled out of her like a mountain stream from melted snow. "Even then, we would have had enough for a fine little farm in Ireland if we ran it sensibly. Mason and I had plans to divide the land between us, raise crops, animals, and our families. Maybe even buy more land adjacent to ours once we became successful." She'd had such solid dreams. The farm almost seemed real to her as did the fields, livestock, and a few marriageable men in her town. She sighed. All gone, now.

"Until?"

Fiona blinked, woken from her daydream. She cleared her throat from the sudden lump forming there. "Until Da gambled our land away, too. Double or nothing, he bet, and we got nothing." She unfolded the dishtowel and began wiping the counter again for something to do with the sudden nervous energy. "So, Mason and I worked, saved, and came to America after Da drank himself to death before our very eyes." Each word hurt as it left her. Giving voice to the pain was said to help a person, but telling John everything had not benefited her after all. Instead, she felt uneasy and ill as if she'd betrayed a trust given to her by someone already gone and unaware of the bond.

John frowned and stared at his boots. "I'm sorry to hear that. It wasn't fair to either one of you."

"Suppose not." She stacked the cooking pot on top of the larger wash pan full of dishes. Picking them up, she held the triangle of cookware against her so the load steadied against her. She rested her chin on the top edge of the pot. "Still, what's done is done. There's no need for sympathy now and, anyway, I'll need to clean up for tomorrow."

John pushed away from the countertop. "Let me help?" He opened the back kitchen door. "I can carry something."

She lifted her chin and he took the top pot from her. "I don't know if you need to help too much." She followed him outside. "I'm capable of doing this myself."

He closed the door behind them and trailed her. "You are, but I never mind talking with a pretty girl."

Fiona set the tub of dishes on the ground with a laugh. She took the cook pot and cleaned it first as to give them to have a place to put the scrubbed dishes. A little part of her heart fluttered at him wanting to spend time with her, but a large part of her mind knew to be wary of his motives. The last thing she needed was a reputation as a loose woman. She needed respectable work, not some shady saloon gal sort of employment. Being direct by telling him to scram might make him angry, and he'd go telling the stationmaster about her sass and she'd lose her job. Giving him a smile, she teased, "Now I know you're after something. Complimenting me and offering to do my chores? Whatever you want, the answer is no."

A familiar rider stepped from around the corner of the barn, distracting her and John both. Fiona smiled. She'd known Randall for a few weeks. He'd been easy on the eyes and pleasant enough that she enjoyed it when he stopped there overnight. She stepped forward, glad to see him. "Hello, stranger, nice of you to show up at long last. There's plenty of work for me to do and for you to interrupt."

He pressed a hand to his chest dramatically and stepped forward to Fiona and John. "What? I wasn't gone for more than a week, and I'd be glad to help you do anything." Giving a nod to John, he said, "Hello, I'm Randall Tate."

"Name's John Williamson." He shook Randall's offered hand. "Pleased to meet you."

She took a dish from the tub and began washing, her thoughts on the men milling about. The two men had the same job but they were very different. Randall had this determined air as if he'd planned every move ages ago. Meanwhile, John was just here in the moment and not really intending on going anywhere else. Maybe. She'd have to think about both men a little more. People watching, comparing and contrasting, and seeing patterns in unrelated things were all fun to her.

Fiona set the clean plate on the water trough's corner. The two men were talking about people they knew in common. None of the names were familiar so she looked up at the evening sky. The stars were the same here as at home, but her hopes and dreams were different. She watched as a star began twinkling. It was too late to make a wish on the first star, besides, wishes were for children who believed in magic. Now the dreams and wishes she had were practical ones. She planned on working until she had a little nest egg, buying a store, and working more until the egg grew into enough to leave her financially secure.

Randall tapped her on the shoulder and pulled her out of the daydream. After a glance at him, she handed him the dish to dry. She'd love to have help from a strong man like him. Only, she also wanted someone to love who wanted the family she'd like to have, too. Her face heated when she glanced from one man to the other. Both were handsome and seemed nice, but then there were a lot of men out in the wild part of America. No need to settle down any time soon.

Randall took her apron from where she'd draped it on the wash pail and began drying. "I reckon you're from back east?" He gave the dish to John to hold and took a fork.

"I am."

As soon as Randall finished with the utensil, he took another plate to dry. "I wasn't interrupting anything earlier, was I?"

"You're always welcome to stop my washing up from dinner." She held out a wet hand to Randall who wiped her hands on her apron. She laughed at the tickling across her palm and said, "At least this time, you're helping while you're talking."

He glanced at John and tilted his head toward Fiona. "She mocks me. You're a witness." He put a dried fork into the clean cooking pot. "Did you hear that the crazy fool riding from one end of the Express to the other reached St. Joseph?"

"No," Fiona said and gave him a clean plate. "Will he be coming back west, then?"

"Doesn't look like it, unless his new bride comes with him."

She remembered meeting him when he passed through. At the time, he'd behaved like a man on a mission. She'd had no idea he'd been riding across for a woman. Wanting a man who loved her as much belonged firmly in the dreams and wishes category. She didn't need someone like him. Not at all. "Oh, that's lovely. He seemed like such a nice young man."

Randall nudged her with his shoulder. "Clay isn't much younger than we are, you know."

The touch embarrassed her a little bit with its intimacy in front of John. She wondered at the odd feeling and stammered, "I suppose not." He had a point about the age differences. In her mind, Clay's hope and enthusiasm gave him a younger demeanor. She held out the last dish for Randall to take and dry. "Sometimes I feel more like a mother to the riders than a friend. Most of them are so young."

"Go on. As if you're not a young lady yourself." Randall grinned at John and said, "She's hardly old enough to be an aunt, never mind our mother. Isn't that right?"

John began to reply until one of the other riders came up to him and asked, "Hey, we're starting a game. Are you in?"

After looking from Fiona to Randall, he said, "Maybe."

"Murphy's playing," the young man added.

"Aw hell. I can't resist winning Murph's money," he muttered. "Yeah, deal me in." He turned to Fiona and said, "A pleasure talking with you, and thank you for a wonderful dinner. I'll take these inside." He picked up the full washtub and, on his way into the station house, hollered back, "Good to meet you, Tate, and join us if you can."

"We'll see," Randall muttered.

Fiona gave him a sharp look. He didn't sound happy at all. With his angry stance and eyebrows meeting in the middle, he didn't appear happy, either. She trusted Randall's opinion. He'd been her first male friend in America and had always been a good person. Did he not think John was a worthy colleague? Her heart sunk a little at the thought of John not being as decent of a man as he seemed. "What do you think about him?"

"It doesn't matter." He turned to examine her. "I care far more about your opinion than I ever will his, and I'd like to know what you think about him?"

His non-answer irritated her even as she appreciated his valuing her opinion before he would man's. She looked back at the station house. What should she tell him? About how she cared for him but John made her heart feel bubbly when he smiled? Or how she liked Randall's solid nature but the other man's restlessness intrigued her? She didn't want to confess anything committal just yet and hedged with her answer. "You're both fine men and seem decent. Other than that, I'm not sure what I think.

CHAPTER TWO

John opened his eyes to the sound of someone snoring. Like him, all the riders slept in bunk rooms, away from where he guessed Fiona slept. He sat up and stared at Randall in the pre-dawn light. He'd bet buckshot to biscuits he was the one making the racket. Sure enough, the other rider let out a snort and rolled over onto his side. John frowned. Of course, the noisiest person in the room would be sound asleep while he was awake and couldn't get back to sleep. After pushing off the covers, he stood and stretched.

He stepped around the other three pony boys on their various pallets and beds. Scents of breakfast already wafted from the kitchen and so he followed his nose. Fiona was at the stove, stirring eggs in a pan. When she glanced over at him, he smiled. "Good morning. You're making me hungry."

"I'm glad. Maybe the smell will wake the others, too."

She seemed a little frazzled this morning with her hair in a long braid down her back, and tendrils framing her face. Every time she favored him with a look from those gorgeous green eyes, his heart skipped a beat. He couldn't help but smile. "My bet is Randall's snoring will do the job first."

"Is that why you're awake, or are you anxious to be on the next horse?"

John walked over to stand closer. "It is, but I'm also ready to ride this morning."

She stirred the eggs before pushing them to one side. "Not before breakfast, though, right?"

"No ma'am. Never before I eat."

After giving him a grin, she nodded at the coffee pot. "You can help yourself. Cups are in the cupboard. And if you'd like to offer help, I'd appreciate your setting the table."

"I suppose I could." John took and filled a cup with coffee. He grabbed a stack of dishes with his free hand and put them on the dining room table. When he came back into the kitchen, he asked, "Will you have breakfast with us?"

She laid a few pieces of thick bacon in the pan. "I'd like to but no. I'll eat something fast before starting supper."

Breakfast was still on the stove and she was planning dinner already? "So soon?"

"Afraid so." She put in the last strip of bacon. "Some riders have an early dinner while others need to eat much later in the day. I like to keep food ready for them."

John leaned against the doorframe, ready to ask about cold dinners for riders in a hurry. Randall walked in and stopped him before he could start. The taller young man went over to Fiona as if John weren't in the room.

"Good morning to the loveliest lass this side of the Mississippi." He kissed her cheek.

John grit his teeth and tried to ignore the slight tug of jealousy in his mind; Fiona was a little flushed after glancing at him. He loosened his jaw and tried to appear disinterested. Which, he was. She was pretty and he already liked her a lot more than any other woman. But not so much as to care if another man greeted her in a far too friendly way. Other riders might be bothered if a gal they wanted to talk with enjoyed a kiss or two from Randall. Not him. He didn't care.

"We have company."

Randall turned to look where she nodded and his smile faded when his and John's eyes met. "Good morning to you, too. Sorry if I don't compliment you on your beauty."

John couldn't help but grin despite the twinge of envy. "No apologies necessary or wanted." He held up the plates for a second. "If you'll excuse me?" he said and escaped to the dining room so his face couldn't betray him any more.

After he set the dishes in their places, he paused before going back into the kitchen. The two were talking and laughing. He couldn't hear distinct words as much as the friendliness between the pair.

He stood by the table and stared out through the window on the opposite wall. Last night's poker game had probably nixed any chance he might have had of a friendship with the lovely Fiona. She'd just finished telling him about her father's gambling ways before he'd run off to play cards. Would telling her how he never bet every penny in his pocket help or hurt her opinion of him? Part of him wanted to confess while the other part didn't want to hear anything negative from her.

A rider walked between him and the window, and John shook himself from the daydream. He nodded a greeting to the man and went back to the kitchen for silverware and coffee cups. He needed to stay focused on his true mission and not get calf-eyed over some Irish gal.

Only, when John walked into the room and caught her laughing, he wished she'd been amused by something he'd said. Fiona and Randall seemed engrossed in each other as he gathered the remaining table settings. Neither acknowledged him as Randall stood uselessly by while Fiona finished plating up the food.

John reached out to take the coffee pot to the table, but before he could catch hold of the handle, Randall picked up the container. "Hey, buddy. You set the table for us. Let me help the lady, too."

She shook her head at them and patted Randall's shoulder. "No need to fuss. Breakfast is ready so have a seat."

He followed Fiona and Randall out into the dining room. Her brother was sitting with two pony boys and Bill, the station's owner. John watched as Fiona placed the food in the middle of the table. No other women ate with the workers or he'd be the first to suggest she share the meal with them.

Fiona glanced at John and smiled when their eyes met. "Since we have an extra person, would you please pull up one of the other chairs while I get your setting?"

The dining area wasn't large but it was big enough for the table and a couple of spare chairs. John dragged one over and two of the boys parted to let him sit. As he settled in, Fiona reappeared with his dish, a knife and a fork rolled in a napkin, and a coffee cup. "Thank you, ma'am."

She set everything down in front of him and refreshed his coffee. The other boys joined in with a low "Wooo," as she did so. She shook her finger at them. "Now, now, none of that." She turned to John. "This is why I keep to myself. Less trouble."

He grinned as she left the room. The other men resumed their conversation but he didn't bother to listen. Instead, he had half a mind to pick up and join her in the kitchen. He looked around at the other men and decided to wait until she needed help washing dishes. Otherwise, they'd see him sneaking off like a fox toward a henhouse and tease him. He didn't mind a little bit of kidding around, but Fiona might not appreciate the joshing about his interest in her.

A horn sounded outside, distant, signaling the approach of another rider. Randall stood up while wiping his mouth. "My turn to go." He tossed down the napkin.

Fiona walked in with another basket. "So soon?" At his nod, she grabbed a couple of rolls before setting down the basket. "You'll want something for later." She wrapped the bread up in his discarded napkin.

"Thank you, darlin'. You're the only reason to visit so far east," he said and gave her a quick kiss on the cheek. He was gone before the boys stopped hollering catcalls at him.

Fiona stared after him with a hand on her cheek as

if to keep the kiss against her skin. John frown, puzzled by his anger over the small gesture. He looked over at Mason for a gut check on his own emotions. Mason seemed equally displeased by the kiss, if one went by the way he stabbed at his eggs.

John suppressed a grin and picked up a piece of bacon. If her brother wasn't too happy at how fresh Randall had been with Fiona in front of everyone, then John didn't need to be happy about it, either. He waited, wanting to catch her in the kitchen alone and ask what she felt for the man. Eating slowly and downing one too many rolls, he struggled to stay until the last man left the table. He began clearing up the dishes almost before the last pony boy's butt left the chair.

Fiona walked in just as he finished gathering the silverware. "Goodness! You don't need to do my work for me." She hurried over and took the stack of plates from him. "Thank you very much. Keep this up and I'll be riding ponies while you're serving up food for everyone." She turned and went to the kitchen.

John followed her with a finger through the cup handles in one hand, and the silverware in the other. He entered the kitchen in time to see her place the dishes into the washtub. He said, "I don't mind helping a little. I'd do the same for my Ma at home."

"You're good to your mother then." She took the silverware, needing both of her smaller hands to his single large one. They went into the tub and she carefully accepted the ceramic cups from him. "Your help is much appreciated but you have your job and I have mine."

He shrugged and struggled to remember what his

usual casual attitude felt like. Seems like his easygoing outlook had faded into nothing since they'd met. "There's nothing to do until the next horse east."

"Very well. If you're packed and ready to ride, I suppose I don't mind having someone to talk with while I'm washing." She picked up the tub. "Grab that towel and I'll let you dry."

John laughed. "Let me?"

"Yes, it's not a privilege I let just anyone have, you know." She turned and left the room with him trailing behind. Holding the door, she added, "You've not been clumsy so far, so I trust you with my plates."

He couldn't resist teasing as they went to the water pump. "Your plates, hmm?"

She gave him a slight smile and shrugged. "I might be taking too much ownership in my work."

"After the meals I've had so far, the Express is lucky to have you." He sat on the edge of the water trough and enjoyed the twinkle in her eyes.

Fiona chuckled while filling the pan with water. "You don't say?" She picked up a cup and quickly washed it in the running water. "Keep sweet talking me and I'll begin to take you as seriously as I do Randall."

John grabbed the clean cup she offered to him and began drying it. "You're not as interested in him as he seems to be in you, are you?"

Her mouth opened and closed as if she didn't know how to answer. A horn sounded to the west and her face brightened. She almost hopped up and down in glee as she said, "I'd love to answer you but I think you'd best be going."

Next time, he thought while dampening down his

impatience. They could talk a lot more about their life goals when he came by again. John nodded. "You're right, that's my signal to go. I'll bring a large bowl for your clean dishes when I come back." He ran up to the station to grab his knapsack, an apple, and her bowl.

"Just go and be careful. There've been several Indian attacks," she hollered as he went into the house.

Her news made him pause for a couple of seconds before rushing on to his room. More attacks? Several stations to their east had been burned down, rebuilt, and burned again. People and livestock had died each time. He shrugged off the fear gripping him. Signing up to be a rider meant carrying the mail no matter what or who tried to stop them.

CHAPTER THREE

John hurried to his bunk and grabbed his knapsack, slinging it over his head and shoulder. He slowed while running through the kitchen and grabbed a bowl for Fiona. The other pony boy arrived so he didn't let her take time to thank him. Her smile was enough for him as he approached the station keeper, Bill, who was holding the fresh mount. When the exhausted horse stopped, he took the mail's mochila from one saddle and laid it over the other.

As soon as the mail settled on the leather saddle with a squeak, John hopped on and took off toward the next station. He'd been back and forth on this run several times, the road followed Carson River's north bank to Miller's Station. The road, while flat in most parts, ran between the river and intermittent bluffs. An occasional stagecoach kicked up dust, and John squinted to keep the dirt out of his eyes.

Soon, he approached two small buildings, though the nearby stable equaled both of them put together. He let out a yell and a grizzled old man hobbled out of one of the buildings.

John stopped the horse and hopped down. "Howdy."

"Eh," he grunted back while throwing over the mochila. "Indians have been quiet around here lately. Don't expect that to last long."

"I'll keep my eyes open," he replied as the old man turned and made his way to the stable with a tired horse in tow.

He hawed at the fresh mount and they took off for the next station. The newly built Fort Churchill wasn't much further along, he almost wanted to keep going but an angry growl from his stomach nixed that idea. He let out a holler when seeing the log cabin in among the trees.

The middle-aged man leading a horse up to the road looked familiar. As he approached, John grinned. Clem had won a lot of wooden chips from him in the last card game they'd played. He skidded the horse to a stop and dismounted. "Hello, there. Spent all the wooden nickels I gave you?"

He laughed and handed the fresh horse's reins to John. "Sure did. Some greenhorn came by and took them off my hands." Clem settled the mochila in place. "You coming back this evening? I can cut up a few more for you to lose by tonight."

John chuckled. "Hadn't planned on it. I might let the boys at Cold Springs skin me instead."

Clem shook his head. "Shame. I need to practice my winning."

"Later, then," John said, nudging the horse in the flank. The two took off before John remembered he'd wanted to rest at that station. He crouched down some and urged the horse on a little faster. Dinner would just taste that much better by the delay.

He said, "Hyah," to the horse to urge him on before spitting out the bug that flew in, remembering why he kept his mouth shut on a run. If he'd been thinking before leaving Carson City, he'd have asked Fiona to pack a couple of breakfast rolls for him, too.

Fiona doing anything for Randall bothered the heck out of him and he didn't want to know why. There was no need for him to dwell on changing his mind about anything, he didn't need to settle down with any gal. Plenty of women waited for him in Sacramento for when he quit the Express.

Another stagecoach rolled by, kicking up a plume of dust, and he sneezed as he rode through the cloud. All right, so maybe not a lot of women. Or not even one. He adjusted his knapsack where it rubbed against his shoulder. He might not meet the girl he'd marry until the next year or ten. John planned on waiting until his thirties to marry. His ma would have a fit if he told her, but, he refused to stop his carefree life any sooner than he wanted. The girl he'd one day marry was probably living in another country right now. Before finding her way to Sacramento, she'd live somewhere far away and exotic.

Like Ireland.

"Poo!" he hollered to only the horse. "Not Ireland and not Fiona." He stretched his neck one way and then another. No. The woman might be charming, pretty, and attractive with her accent, but he had serious plans of doing nothing. Fiona was far too industrious for him.

He slowed his horse as the road grew more uneven with potholes full of sand. Crossing this stretch of road would be trouble for a coach or wagon, John imagined. They'd have to slow down and swerve to keep from getting stuck in the road's depressions. The stages he'd passed had been in a hurry to make up for lost time. He didn't blame them. The closer he rode to Sand Springs station, the more sand drifts they encountered.

Last time he passed this way, he made the mistake of moving off the trail for an approaching stagecoach. His horse sunk hock deep into the sand, they were both lucky the animal didn't break a leg from the abrupt stop. Plus, he learned sand wasn't so bad to land on when falling from horseback.

John glanced down at the horse's mane. In the sunlight, the warm umber color reminded him of Fiona's hair, which, he refused to think about. The sagebrush on either side of the road weren't as clear green as her eyes but had a silvery cast to them. While the light brown soil they galloped over might be the same dark tan as her freckles, he wasn't reminded of her.

Judging by the drifts encroaching upon the road, Cold Springs should be ahead if the huge sand dunes were still the station's marker. As he approached, he saw they'd begun rebuilding new walls. Black rock came up halfway on a new wooden frame. Smart, since Indians had burned down the last building. The Paiutes attacked this leg of the Express enough to keep the employees in a cycle of rebuilding. From what he could tell, Cold Springs had rebuilt using stone walls as a defense. Too late for the last couple of men killed there. Even as he rode closer to the place, John didn't see anyone around.

What if the station had been attacked yet again and he came upon the victims as they lay there? A chill went through him despite the hot afternoon. He hadn't seen someone dead since his Pa died. He nudged the horse into resuming a gallop. After the first few miles of worry, he'd relaxed and been able to dwell on Fiona and the attraction he had for her. The various attacks and killings at various stops hadn't seemed real until now, when he faced a newly abandoned station.

He let out a holler and a station keeper brought out the fresh horse. He pulled the animal to a stop and said, "Howdy," as a lanky but short young man hurried up to them.

"I can take the next run if you don't mind," the rider said.

His muscles and bones feeling far older than usual left John jumping off the horse with stiff legs. It was a good sign he'd been wise to plan on staying here until tomorrow. "Not at all. I'm ready to stop for the night."

As soon as the mochila hit the saddle, the next rider was up and gone. John turned to the other man. "I don't reckon you all have a good cook around here?"

The station hand chuckled and turned to lead the tired horse to food and water in a pen next to the stable. "Afraid not. Word is, the best cook is out west of here at Carson City."

John narrowed his eyes while following him to the stable. The man meant Fiona. His Fiona, or maybe not his entirely, but certainly a woman he'd claim as his own. The station hand pulled the saddle from the horse with a grunt. After looking at the man more objectively, John relaxed. He seemed a lot closer to being Fiona's father's age than a suitor should be. "You've been out there, then?"

"Lord, no." He nodded toward the station house and removed the horse's bit and bridle. "She's what all the boys in there talk about. Don't worry, you'll hear about her soon enough once you're inside." The man began ambling toward the station house as John stared after him.

He. Didn't. Care. Let the others speculate on the Irish gal all they wanted. He had plans to enjoy life until some woman convinced him otherwise. He shifted his knapsack to the opposite side and headed for the outhouse. Once done, he couldn't find a water pump within eyesight near the house or stable. He figured the corral at the base of a hill had to be close to a creek. Especially since several trees snaked a path alongside the wooden fence. Certain he'd find a spring to clean his face and hands in, John walked down to the corral.

As he reached the trickle of a stream, a southeast wind brought the smell of beef cooking. His stomach growled in response. Seemed he had arrived at the best time, unless they'd already eaten and the wind was just kidding with him. In that case, he hoped they'd be like Carson City and have cold foods available. He'd have to wait until dinner for something to eat if they didn't.

John kneeled and washed his face and hands in the cold spring water. Cleaning his hot skin felt good. He took a few sips of the water and was delighted when the drink tasted as fresh as it felt. Not wanting to waste the chance, he took his canteen out of his knapsack and refilled it from the stream. His stomach growled again, whether from the cold water or hunger, John wasn't sure. He stood and put away his canteen before heading back to the home station.

Unlike the more peaceful stations to the west, windows here were chinks cut out in the stone for rifles to poke through during attacks. He opened the door and stepped inside. Several pony boys sat around a table. As he approached, John welcomed the refreshing cooler air after being in the desert heat all day. Sunlight streamed in through the slats while dust hovered and swirled in the spotlight, illuminating how the stove had a pile of dirty dishes on it. The table was no better with one of the men resting his feet on the surface. John felt sure the man's socks had been white at some time but were now a dirty gray brown.

"Looks like we have a new player." One of the men laid down his cards and stood. "The name's Jim. There's Rob, Bart, and Hyatt. You hungry?"

"Nice to meet you, and yeah. Carson City was a ways back." Cots were lined up on the far side of the room. Curtains hung on either side, separating the large area into two smaller ones. He went over to claim a bed for himself by laying his knapsack on top.

Several of the men began grinning. Bart stood up first. "I suppose I'd better see if Chuck is done flipping steaks for us."

He ambled off and Jim motioned for John to take the empty chair. "Indians came by last night and helped themselves to our few head of cattle. We fought them off but killed one in the process."

"Indians' loss is our supper," Rob said. "You don't think Bart'd mind if we reshuffled and dealt a new game?"

Hyatt peeked at the absent man's cards. "Probably not, since he was losing." Footsteps stomped out and the tilted cards smacked against the table.

Bart frowned before grabbing the end of a bench. The feet scraped along the dirt floor. "Dang it, Hyatt! Stop doing that or I'll have to shoot you."

"Eh, you'd have done the same."

He scooped up his now not so secret hand. "That's the only reason you're not bleeding out on the floor right now." Pushing his cards toward the middle with the others, he added, "Chuck says if you like your steaks mooing at you, you'd better get on out there." He nodded at the stacked dishes. "You might want to grab the plate you want and clean it up, too."

Cards forgotten, each pony rider grabbed a dirty plate, silverware, and followed each other to the creek that gave Cold Springs its name.

Bart said, "Too bad we don't have a cute little filly out here to cook and clean for us like some stations do."

John frowned at Bart while kneeling at the water. "Sounds like you have someone in mind."

A chorus of chuckles sounded before Jim said, "Naw, just that little ole gal in Carson City. She's one of the prettiest girls I've ever seen."

Hyatt splashed water on Rob and said, "If it weren't for that brother of hers ready to whup some butt, I'd have started courting her by now."

"Yeah?" Jim dug down and scrubbed the crusted dish with a handful of river sand. "How do you know Randall hasn't asked her to marry him by now?"

"He hasn't," John said and got to his feet with a clean dish, fork, and knife. They all turned to look at him and he added, "Not since yesterday, anyway."

Rob squinted and held up a hand to block the sun behind John, and asked, "You saw her, then?"

"You haven't?" Bart chided while shaking water from his dishes. "You're missing out."

"I try to make it as far as Carson Station," Hyatt began. He and the others chimed in with their agreements as they made their way back to the house. "Sometimes I'm headed east and don't get to see her for a couple of weeks."

Reaching the station house first, Rob opened the door for everyone else. "How long has she been in Carson?"

Jim answered before John could. "Not too long." He looked at Bart and added, "A couple of months maybe?"

Bart nodded and found a seat at the table. "Since spring."

John sat, too. He didn't like them gossiping about Fiona, but figured he'd learn more about her this way. As long as they didn't turn to crudeness about her, he'd let them tell him all they knew. He knew why she and Mason had left home but wanted to hear if these men knew her story, too. "She left Ireland for a good reason, I suppose," he offered and took a bite of the steak.

Jim swallowed and said, "She and her brother made their way west on the stage until stopping there."

"Either the money ran out or the job sounded good enough to stay," Bart added.

John shrugged and hoped the others would chime in, too. "Maybe a little bit of both."

Hyatt swallowed and held out his plate for more.

"We should play for her."

"What?" Shocked, John spoke a little louder than he'd intended. Part of it was due to the suggestion they'd play for Fiona, the rest of it was from how the young man had all but inhaled his food. "How?"

"Easy," Hyatt said before cutting up his steak. "Pick the game to play and let's gamble to see who should be courting her."

John's hand trembled as he gave Chuck his plate for more. Fiona would be furious enough with them gambling. He couldn't imagine the explosion her temper would create if she knew they were playing for her affections. He didn't need to try and see if she had a temper to match her hair and heritage. "No. We're not gambling for a woman. I won't allow it."

Chuck put another steak on Rob's plate. Hyatt and Burt began laughing while Jim frowned. Rob looked from one group to the other, and then at John and said. "I don't think anyone asked for your permission."

Some of them may have met Fiona but it didn't mean they knew her as a person. Heck, he didn't feel all that familiar with her himself, yet figured any woman finding out her best guy won her on a bet, or worse, lost her on a bet, would be unhappy. John glared at each man as if they'd already hurt Fiona's feelings by suggesting the wager. He'd play their stupid game and he'd win if only so none of them could court her. "Fine. If that's the way you want it. I'm in." He stood with a couple of the other men. "And, I play to win."

"That's the only way to go," Hyatt replied with a grin. "I'm finishing my dinner first. Good cooking, Chuck."

"Thank ya. I'll make jerky out of the rest, I reckon."

John ignored the conversation between Jim and Rob on his way back to the spring with them. He'd wash up, put away his dishes, and win the game, easy as pie. As they approached, a few songbirds gave a cry of protest and flew off to some nearby stunted trees further up the ravine. Cleaning his plate and silverware didn't take long. He took a few sips of water and looked around at the long shadows of early evening. Alone, he looked back to see the other two filing back into the house after barely rinsing their dishes. No wonder the place was a mess, the boys here didn't clean as they went.

A shout from the west rang out as a rider approached. John shielded his eyes from the glare of the sun hovering over the horizon. As both he and the rider approached the station, Chuck stepped out to saddle up a fresh horse. He went in the back door to find Rob, Hyatt, Burt, and Jim seated at the table already, their dishes stacked in the wash pail.

Rob spoke first. "You just washed your plate? We'd let you clean ours, too, if you'd said something."

John pulled back a chair and sat. "I'm sure you ladies would, but I'm not your momma."

The others laughed as Rob shuffled. The cards made a soft ruffle in his hands. "That's a fact, even if you might be as pretty as her."

He couldn't keep from grinning while shaking his head. "Just shut up and deal."

CHAPTER FOUR

After a few seconds of studying his cards, John glanced up at the others. Somehow, he suspected Randall would be the true winner of Fiona's heart no matter who won. He didn't figure on ever having a chance with her with that yahoo around. And now? He held a straight flush in hearts, a winning hand in nearly any game. But, did he want to win her heart at all or was he just competing for competition's sake? If she did fall in love with him, what then? Marriage, a home, a crowd of babies?

The thought stopped him cold. He hesitated in calling his hand. Rob was grinning at him, he scowled in return. A man needed time to think before gambling away his future, and none of these pony huggers gave him any space to ponder his options.

Rob waved his hand of cards. "You gonna call or sit and think about losing all night?"

"I'm calling." John placed his cards on the table. "Straight flush and I'd better comb my hair tomorrow before I see her again."

After a laugh, Rob shook his head. "Too bad,

buddy." He laid down a royal flush in spades. "The lovely Fiona O'Brien is my girl, not yours."

"You sure she's not already wrapping Randall around her little finger?" Burt quipped.

Hyatt nudged John. "Heck, I'd like to be anywhere near her, never mind wrapped around anything."

The slight push from Hyatt knocked John out of his shocked stupor. He'd lost with a straight and worse, lost the contest to see Fiona as a suitor? Both were bad and, after giving the other man a glare, he said, "Watch yourself. She's a lady." The men here could hoot and holler all they liked. At the end of the day, he'd see to it that they respected her.

"I know, I know." He sighed. "Don't mean any disrespect. She's just pretty, that's all."

Burt tossed in his cards with the others. "Eh, you know it don't matter what we play. I've seen how she looks at Randall, all sweet and nice like."

John didn't need to hear his thoughts echoed outside of his head. He stood, just catching his chair from falling back. "Ma always said all's fair in love and war. Until she's married, we have as good a chance as any."

Rob stretched and grinned before moseying over to his bed for the night. "You mean I have as good a chance, since I won and all. You lost, remember?"

He tried to smile despite the cold lump of anger in his chest. "I have a feeling you're not gonna let me forget."

"Damn straight," Rob replied as one boot hit the floor, then the other. "I play to win and I'll win Fiona, too."

John frowned before going to the back of the room

and settling in on a cot. "Do you even want her?"

"Do you have eyes in your head?" Burt said with a snort. "She's the prettiest thing this side of the Mississippi."

He shrugged while undoing his belt to avoid sleeping on the metal buckle and sat. "How do you know she's the prettiest for sure? You met all the women of a marriageable age around here?"

Burt lay back on his bed with his hands cradling his head. "Not all of them, but a few."

"She won't like your saying she's ugly," Hyatt said while getting onto his cot, shoes and all.

John frowned. With his luck, one of these yahoos would tell Fiona about how he thought she was bad looking. He had to stop this train from leaving the station. He said, "I'd never tell a gal she's ugly, not even second hand. Fiona's a beauty but not the only one. You could find—" He closed his mouth before the next thought could be voiced. Did he really want to say Rob could find a prettier woman when he didn't believe one existed? The men in the room had nothing to do but ride, sleep, eat, and gossip. Which one they enjoyed most was a toss-up, but if he admitted feelings for Fiona? He'd be better off taking out an ad in the Sacramento newspaper so she wouldn't be as likely to know about his interest in her. "Well, never mind. Just know you'd be able to find your own woman without having to fight me for her."

Rob laughed and turned on his side toward everyone else. "Don't mind him, boys. He's just sore at losing a game."

"Sure. That's it," John agreed. "I thought I had it won is all." He put his hands behind his head in a casual pose he didn't quite feel. "Unlike Rob, I have a lot more living to do before hitching my rope to any post."

The room fell silent. Chuck turned down the lantern he'd lit during the game before finding his bunk. John grinned at the lack of a retort from Rob or anyone else. Mentioning marriage stopped the courting talk dead, it seemed, and he almost laughed at their reaction. The idea of something permanent was as anthemia to them, too, huh? He didn't blame them and had to twist the idea in a little harder so none of them got ideas about Fiona. "Yeah, no more card games, drinking, riding off to wherever we want. Instead, it's coming home when the little woman tells you to, sleeping in only one bed, regular dinner times when she says they'll be, thank you very much."

"Huh. I sorta like what you're saying," Burt said. "Fancy that."

Jim came back from outside, closed the door, and went to his bed. "You all still talking about that little ole gal? I figured we'd have something new to play for by now."

Burt propped up his head on one elbow. "Yeah, John here is telling us all about marrying her and how great we'd have it as her husband."

Rob piped up, too. "Yeah, makes me glad I'm a winner."

None of the conversation was going his way. He felt like a dog in the manger with Fiona as the hay. Just because he wanted to wait before marrying anyone didn't mean he'd be fine with someone marrying her. He grumbled to all of them, "Well, marrying anyone sounds like hell to me. A woman tying one of us down isn't worth it, even if the rope she's using is a lovely copper."

Hyatt sighed. "I wouldn't mind a nice golden rope, myself. One who could cook like a dream and knew how to raise the best chickens."

"See if she has a sister," Burt suggested.

Chuck stirred with a cough. "Mornin's going to be here awful early, fellas."

John turned over and faced Hyatt with a good idea. "Plus, morning would be a good time to have a rematch. See if anyone can create a royal flush out of thin air again."

Groans filled the room before Rob said, "I won. You lost, fair and square. Find another gal to hanker for because Fiona's mine."

***

Fiona wiped the crumbs from the stove to her hand with a rag while Mason went on and on about which station had the best horse. "Um hm, that's bad," she said in an automatic response to a negative tone in his voice. He'd been chattering for a half hour now while waiting for the next mail run. He'd spent his time following her around while she cleaned up from breakfast and did dishes. Like the other men around here, her brother was full of everyone's business but his own. She'd tried to redirect him into more useful topics than gossip provided, but he'd stubbornly wanted to talk about everything unimportant in either one of their lives.

She dipped a corner of the rag in a bit of wash water lining the bottom of a bucket. And now, he was going on about the food over at Fort Churchill. She'd spoiled him with her cooking, it seemed. Compliments were nice and all but she'd rather him sweep up or at least dry the dishes. She smiled at him before wiping the thin windowsill. "Thank you. I do my best with what I'm given."

Mason sat on the cooking table, lifting his feet for her to sweep under. As she did so, he said, "Appreciate you keeping me a single man, sis."

"My pleasure." Their superstitious mother had warned the both of them to never sweep under someone's feet or they'd never marry. "I expect you to return the favor someday."

He laughed. "That adverse to a husband, then?"

Fiona swept the dust and dirt out through the back door. "No, more like in favor of you helping to clean up."

"Ha. Women's work." He waved a hand at her scowl. "Anyway, as I was saying…."

His continuation of the one-sided conversation gave her time to check the stove's heat. The cooled metal meant she could clean it off before making lunch. "Um hm," she mumbled in response to whatever Mason was saying now. Grease and the perpetual dust never eased up on her efforts for a spotless kitchen.

Not that anyone cared what the room looked like. Maybe Mason did. She glanced at him, he still sat on the cooking table, talking.

Then again, maybe not.

She rinsed the rag of crumbs. Randall would mind; he seemed like the clean sort. He and John were the only men besides her brother to visit her in the kitchen. And John? Like Randall, he seemed too busy looking at her to notice anything else.

She glanced at Mason with a bit of a smirk before resuming her scrubbing. Her face burned a little at the thought of both men interested in her. Certainly, several men talked a lot about how much they liked her. Randall always stopped and gave her his attention, and John did, too, but she'd only just met him. He had a wild and free quality to him Randall didn't seem to share.

She stared through the window, lost in thought. John was the man who rode up on a pony and tucked your heart into his saddle's mochila cabins. The next instant, he would ride away, never to be seen again. He had probably broken hearts from Sacramento to Kansas City. She saw no need to let him have hers, no matter how appealing the man was.

"It was fine until John Williamson fell and broke his neck."

An icy chill swept through her. People died from such falls. Her fingers trembled as she dropped the rag. "He did what?"

"I wanted to see if you were listening." Mason gave her a grin. "Seems like you weren't."

She picked up the rag before facing her brother with her hands on her hips. He always chose the worst things to tease about. "So? Is he dead or are you just mean?"

"Mean. I suppose he's fine. I made it up. Now that I have your attention, though, what did you want to do for Christmas?"

Fiona threw the dirty cloth into a basket by the door. She had a feeling John couldn't truly be dead or her rotten brother would have been a lot sadder. And now he wanted to chat about Christmas? "Goodness,

Mace. You're talking six months away at least. I don't know where you'll be by then."

"I want time to plan and save up for your gift. I also want to make sure I'm somewhere nearby. Family should be together."

"I agree." She wetted a new washcloth with the last bit of water from breakfast. Wiping down the low cabinet he leaned against, she added, "And I'll give some thought over the coal I'll pick out just for you."

Mason grinned. "I have an equally wonderful gift in mind for you." He paused as a hoof beats pounded outside toward the station, letting them know a rider had arrived. "I'm going on the next run. In the meantime, think about Christmas, would you?"

Before she could give him a good retort, Randall walked in. "Good morning."

Her brother hopped down from the countertop and slung his leather bag over his shoulder. "I suppose I should get going."

"I'm a little early, you have several minutes before needing to leave, yet." He went over to Fiona. "How's my girl doing?"

"I don't know. How is she?" Fiona quipped while Mason rolled his eyes. She raised her eyebrows at her brother and asked Randall, "How was your ride here?"

"Same ole. Dust, the pony, and getting the mail in on time." Randall kissed her cheek. "I'll go clean up and come back to see you." He glanced at Mason. "Have a good one."

Mason nodded. "Will do."

Fiona stood there, stunned at his open affection and rubbing her face with cold fingertips. "What on earth made him do such a silly thing?"

"Hmm. More importantly, does he know you're sweet on another rider?"

Her mouth dropped open and stayed for a couple of seconds before she recovered enough to say anything. "I'm not!" she tried to deny.

"No reaction or feelings for John Williamson?" He pointed at her. "Ah ha! Look at that smile. Don't worry." He kissed her opposite check. "I'll let you tell the both of them about who you prefer yourself."

CHAPTER FIVE

Fiona threw another handful of dried corn to the hens. The birds clucked to each other while pecking for their dinner. Good thing Mason was gone by noon, his smug attitude grated on her last nerve. He always acted as if he knew her better than she did herself. Maybe he did, but the scoundrel didn't have to be so arrogant in his knowledge. She unclenched her fist and threw the last bit of feed for the chickens. The kernels left slight indentions in her palm.

She dusted her hands and left the coop. A whoop sounded in the distance and she recognized the voice. "Think of the devil and he appears," she muttered. The rider was a ways off to the east. She had time to tie up the last few leftovers into a cold dinner for the next rider out. She scooped up the feed pail on her way to the kitchen. Their one barrow, creatively named Mr. Pig, would want her to fill the bucket with potato peelings and other discards instead of leaving the container next to the henhouse.

Soon after returning to the kitchen, she had a couple of biscuits, an apple, and a slice of cheese tied up in a handkerchief for the next rider leaving. He rushed through on his way outside, only pausing when she held out the meal. "You'll want this for later."

He slowed a little and grabbed the offering. "Thank you, miss."

Fiona went to the kitchen's back door as soon as he left. She put her hand on the knob and hesitated. Would she seem too eager if she ran out to check on the garden right now? Laundry and cleaning waited for her, but neither involved accidently seeing John. She withdrew her hand. Not that she wanted to see him at all, really.

She shook her head as if to push away the doubts. Running into John would be a happy accident on her way to refilling the bucket with fresh water for the kitchen. Nothing more. She opened the door and stepped out, grabbing the empty pail along the way.

John stood next to the water trough while talking with Bill. He glanced at her, and when their gazes met, her breath caught. His eyes went back to her a second time, his dark browns staring into hers. Despite a rumpled appearance, he seemed confident, his bold stare as he looked from her head to her toes and back again heated her cheeks.

She picked up her skirts a little to step down from the porch without tripping. Her intention was to walk past on her way to the garden, but he didn't let her. As soon as she passed him, John said, "No hello from the prettiest girl on the station?"

"Ha!" She slowed just enough to turn and tease him. "Keep yourself useful by asking the other pretty girl for a greeting. I'm busy."

"There's not another woman here, is there?" John

asked. "One as lovely as you but far more kind to a tired pony boy?"

She laughed. "Sure there is. Wander around until you find her and don't be afraid to go far."

"I'm happy right here," he replied with a grin.

Fiona's heart gave a little flutter when he stared into her eyes. "Well, I suppose that's good." She nodded at Bill to include him into the conversation. "Wouldn't want the riders to have a complaint about the station."

John cut his eyes over at Bill. "I don't have any. Do any other riders?"

"No sir. The food's been better since Miss O'Brien arrived, and the beds smell good again. Only Miss Jenny over at Fort Churchill can compare."

She swung the bucket a little, suddenly shy. "Thank you. I appreciate the compliment." Part of her wondered if they were being nice just to gain extra housekeeping or food from her. The female part of her wanted to believe their compliments. "You all work hard and at all hours of the day and night. Good food and fresh bedding is the least I can do to help the Express run efficiently."

"Careful in how good of a job you do here," John said. "Or every rider will be stopping by."

"They'll need to hire two of you, then," Bill added with a nod. "You're a hard working young lady as it is."

Another pair of female hands might mean more time for her to accomplish smaller tasks like clothes mending or a true spring cleaning of the station. "I don't suppose I'd mind a little help."

John held out his hands in a welcoming gesture. "All you have to do is ask. I'm sure me or some others around here wouldn't mind helping for a smile or two from you."

Fiona couldn't help but grin at his suggestion. She'd wanted true help, not some pony boys strutting around and trying to impress her. To push him a little to see if he meant what he said, she joked, "Careful, or I'll take you up on the offer."

"Anytime." He nodded toward the house. "And there's another helpful hand for you coming right now."

Randall walked up and put his arm around her. "There you are. I'd been looking for you."

"Oh?" His arm lay heavy on her shoulders. She really wanted to shrug him off of her but didn't want to cause a scene in front of the other men. "What do you need?"

"As much time as you're giving these rascals." He gave her a squeeze. "Or more, if I can."

"Such a tease. I happen to know you're far too busy to help with women's work." She eased away from his touch. Lifting the pail, she added, "I've already been far too long. If you'll excuse me?"

Randall tipped an imaginary hat as he replied, "Of course, ma'am."

From beside Bill, John looked from Randall to Fiona but remained quiet with a slight smile on his face. She knew he'd caught her easing Randall away from being a little too friendly with her. Headed toward the water pump, she didn't need to glance back at the group to know John watched her.

After filling the water bucket, she walked by as the trio moved on. She liked how they were so engrossed in their conversation, none of them called out to her.

So many chores still remained before dinner and she'd already spent way too much time talking.

The kitchen water refreshed, Fiona went to the bedrooms with a dust cloth. Everyone left the windows open in the summer, so the dust accumulated on near everything. She almost didn't mind the extra work. The time spent wiping gave her a chance to make sure the rooms were adequately cleaned. Stripping sheets and making beds in her usual rush didn't give her the same opportunity to really look at what needed fixing or replacing. The riders weren't the best about reporting wear and tear on items, she'd noticed. Even her picky brother kept quiet on small things like a cracked lantern chimney.

Fiona threw bedding from one room out into the hallway before going to the next. John's knapsack laid on the bed. She paused before removing his sheets and pillowcase, doing this for him seemed like an intimate act. She glanced up and out of the window at the low mountains to the west. He'd wanted to settle in Sacramento, hadn't he? For a man with sparse goals, he knew more where he'd end up than she did. A person could own a shop or operate a trading post nearly anywhere in the world, even Sacramento.

She shook her head to refocus on the task at hand. Randall would be a better choice, she reminded herself while throwing the bedding into the hall like before. He was the most solid and dependable man she'd met out here in the States. Plus, his goals matched hers in owning a store someday. John, meanwhile? She shook her head and began wiping down the dusty surfaces. How could anyone go through life without more than a vague idea of where he was going?

Done dusting and loaded up with an armful of sheets, she went to the water trough. The station keeper had frowned upon her using the tank as a washtub. Or, he had until she'd refilled it with fresh water for the horses.

Clean linen soon lined up along the corral's fence. Fiona glanced toward the house. If John and Randall were serious about helping her, she could have them construct a proper clothesline. How on earth anyone survived out here without one was beyond her. She'd have to put faith in the others respecting her laundry drying.

Some of the boys sat on the porch waiting for the next rider to pass by. John and Randall were there with a couple of the usual pony riders and a new man she hadn't met. Randall waved to her first, while John's face lit up as he smiled and gave her a nod. She waved back at both and gave them one last look before turning the barn's corner. John's smile did crazy things to her heart. As soon as their visual link broke, she leaned against the warmed wood of the building. She couldn't remember seeing a better-looking man. He'd seemed as happy to see her as she had been to see him.

She sighed, second-guessing her opinion about Randall being a better fit for her. The other rider was a fine man and a smart woman would focus on him. She stared at the afternoon sky. Her dreams of opening a shop didn't include caring for a restless man-child. Even if the person had an understated charm and seemed to genuinely care about a woman. He teased, sure, but she'd seen enough of the world to discern truth from lies.

John appeared from around the barn and startled

her out of the daydream. She squeaked in surprise. "I'm afraid you caught me lollygagging about…things. Yes, various things." His knowing grin left her face hot with embarrassment. "I mean, not about you in particular or anything."

"All right, not about me, so don't stop lollygagging on my account." He put his hands in his pockets and walked up to her. "I wouldn't want to interrupt your chores."

Fiona chuckled and grabbed at the chance to direct the conversation away from her thinking about him. "You wouldn't stop me from ironing, cooking, or dusting? Not even if I ask you to?"

"Darlin, I'd do anything if you asked."

Biting her lip to keep from laughing at how he wagged his eyebrows, she asked, "Even if I asked you to dig a new outhouse hole for me? And hanging a new clothesline if you're not too tired afterward? Both are part of my chores, after all."

"Sure! I can ask Randall to grab a shovel and get busy."

"Ha, funny. I'm sure he'd love you for volunteering him." She stopped leaning against the barn and made a come on motion. "I'll let you help me harvest vegetables for tonight's dinner."

He fell in step beside her as they walked to the garden. "You'll let me? I'm a lucky man."

"You are, actually." Fiona opened the makeshift gate set into a fence that barely kept the wildlife out. The lack of rain meant she brought water to the plants once a week or so. Settling down to her knees next to an okra plant, she asked John, "Have you had sun warmed tomatoes and fresh shelled peas?"

"No." He waited while she harvested some ready vegetables and took a few spears of okra from her. "I've had apples shaken from the tree and pie made from the day's pumpkin."

"Both sound wonderful." Satisfied nothing was left unpicked, she stood and went to the tomatoes. Several were almost too ripe. Her mouth watered at how good they'd taste freshly picked. She held a particularly beautiful tomato before giving the fruit a slight twist so it would fall into her palm. "I wonder if apple trees could do well out here. I've had to add a bucket or two of water every week to help these plants along." She straightened and gave John the fruit. "A peach tree might be lovely, too."

"A tree is a bit of a commitment. The next cook might not be as diligent as you are." He went over to the yellow squash plant. "I see a couple that are ready over here. I can go ahead and pick them for you."

"Please do and good point about the trees." Fiona went over a row to check for more vegetables. "I'd hate to plant a small orchard only to have them die as soon as I left." She knelt, making sure to let her knees rest on a patch of mulching straw. The green squash needed picking so she took out her pocketknife from her apron and cut several from the plant. "Like you, I can't commit to anyone or anything until I have a bigger nest egg."

John took the extra squash from her and added the vegetable to his collection. He untucked his shirt to use the tail as a basket. "I could if the right opportunity came along."

She glanced up at him. A little bit of his skin showed above his belt line but she glanced away before getting a good look at what his shirt had been hiding. "So could we all, I imagine." She stood and folded her knife before dropping it back into her pocket. "I think that's everything for now. Let's go inside so you're not standing around holding vegetables all day."

He chuckled and followed her out of the small garden. "Talking about opportunities, though, I suppose several chances passed me by, since I wasn't looking to settle down with anyone."

Fiona nodded. She'd met several men who'd be excellent husbands and fathers someday. Just not now and not for her. "I'll bet that's true for everyone. We don't see what we're not looking for." She hurried ahead to open the door for him. "There have been several stores I could have bought but never even noticed because I didn't think I was ready."

John smiled before going on inside. "If I said I never noticed any pretty girl I met, would you believe me?"

Fiona laughed with a snort before covering her mouth for a second or two. Shaking off the embarrassment, she unloaded his shirt for him. "No. I suspect you notice every one of them even if you end up riding off into the sunset alone."

"You know, the sun sets in the west. Exactly where you are." He leaned against the counter to watch her store the vegetables. "A man could be persuaded to stay with a fine lady like you."

She paused in placing the last tomato and glanced over at him. The lazy way he half leaned against the counter and the almost over confident smile bothered her. She couldn't pinpoint why, exactly, but his compliments rang hollow in her ears. Probably from dealing with Da. He'd call her a fine lady when she tried to clean him up from gaming and drinking away the night. Hearing the same words from a younger man didn't change how they affected her. She stood straight and crossed her arms. "Mind telling me why you're really here talking to me and helping so much? Because I don't believe this pig slop of charm you're tossing at me."

CHAPTER SIX

John narrowed his eyes. He didn't intend to be dishonest in how he felt for Fiona. In fact, the more he thought about his feelings, the more he realized how smitten he was with her. Even with her standing there, scowling at him, she was lovely. "Oh? Think I'm lying to you?"

"I don't think you're being truthful, no."

Her thinking he'd lie to her hurt his heart. Not that he was being completely honest, but he wasn't giving her a complete falsehood by complimenting her. He lifted his chin and nodded toward the door. "Very well, if that's your opinion. You're wrong, but I'll leave you to it, then." The more her calling him a liar sank in, the more his hurt slipped into anger. "We've both been in here alone far too long for propriety's sake. Wouldn't want your Randall to worry."

She crossed her arms while frowning at him. "He's not my Randall and don't know if he'll ever be."

In a flash, the meaning behind her words hit him like a cast iron skillet; Fiona didn't trust a man's affections. He tried not to grin at the knowledge. She was smart to not fall for every smooth talker.

The question to him was: who did she have any sort of feelings for, him or Randall? "Going by his actions, he seems to think it'll only be a matter of time before you're in love with him, too." Wanting to add to his casual air, he shrugged. "If I didn't know better, I'd say he's decided your fate."

She lifted her chin. "There's where you're wrong, boyo. No one, not even Mason decides anything for me."

John stared down at the floor to keep from smiling. He couldn't help it if the woman was beautiful when angry. Her flashing green eyes and cute frowning lips tempted him into kissing her happy again. "I don't blame you a bit. You're a free woman with a strong mind of her own. If you wanted to choose anyone but Randall, he'd have to step aside."

"Exactly so."

He tried to not smile at her adorable nod and kept going. "Even if Mason disapproved of the man you fell in love with, too bad. Your life is your own."

"I'm glad you understand."

Two yesses from her and now was the time to make his final point. "And if you wanted me to court you, once you realize I mean it, you'd be the one deciding where we go and what we did together."

She stopped cold before laughing. "That's the truth, even if you're not meaning what you say in the least."

John was beginning to dislike her calling him dishonest. He leaned forward until their noses nearly touched, she didn't move away but stood her ground. He grinned while saying, "Better go get started on the new clothesline and outhouse hole, then."

"Maybe not the outhouse hole just yet," she whispered. "The clothesline is far more important at the moment."

"Very well. I'll let Randall know you're saving outhouse duty for him." He brushed his lips against hers in the briefest of touches. "Until dinner, then."

"Yes," she breathed. "Dinner."

John turned on his heel and left the room. The cards be damned, he wanted to win the game for Fiona for real and forever. Spotting the station keeper at the corral, he hurried over to him.

Bill waited until John was closer to say, "Dang woman. We can't do anything with the horses until her laundry dries."

Hiding a smile at the older man's frustration, John tilted his head and quipped, "Funny you should mention that. I offered to help her by stringing up a clothes line this afternoon."

"Good idea, son." Bill spit out the twig he was chewing on. "I get real tired of having to be careful around here on wash day."

"Then let's fix the problem for all of us." John looked at the stable to see what hung on the outside wall. "I don't know where everything is around here but it seems we'd need some sort of rope and two posts."

"Can't help ya with the posts just yet but we got plenty of rope. Follow me."

John did as Bill suggested and trailed along behind to the barn's tool area. "I don't reckon we could go into town for the posts she needs."

"I'll mark it down on the supply list for next time." He went to the wall and pulled down a coil of rope.

"Let's take this out and measure between the house and nearest building. See how much this'll take."

Holding the end of the coil as Bill walked from the station house to the outhouse reminded John of when he helped his father. The memory dredged up a feeling of homesickness he'd just as soon forget. Pa wasn't coming back, Ma was finally happy, and he had a life of freedom and adventure.

"John, you woolgatherin'?"

He grinned at Bill. "Afraid so. What did I miss?"

"Stay here while I fetch a hammer and nail. We're lucky to have a wood house instead of the stone ones needed in the deserts." Bill hobbled off to the barn. "Don't go nowhere."

"I won't." The wind shifted directions a bit, carrying the scent of Fiona's cooking to him. His stomach growled in response. Just as he started to yell at Bill to hurry, the station keeper left the barn to come back. "We'll need a shovel, too. Miss O'Brien wants me to dig a new hole for the outhouse."

"Does she now?" Bill gave John a wry grin before hammering in the long nail. "Hope no one's nappin' right now." He hit the nail a couple of times more before taking the end of the rope from John. "She's fooling you. I dug a fresh hole last week."

John chuckled and took the coil from Bill as he tied a knot. "I should dig one right close to her vegetable garden and show her what a good job I've done."

"If it weren't a lot of wasted time and effort," he began while hammering in the second nail. "I'd say go ahead. Though, you might have to ride far and fast right after you tell her."

John laughed at the idea of running away from an

angry Irish woman. "I'd make sure the next rider was in sight before saying anything."

"Smart man," Bill said and took the strung-out rope from him. He measured the rope out enough for a knot and some spare before cutting with his pocket knife. "She's a good one, though. Deserves a decent man who'll appreciate her."

"Like Randall?" John ventured. He wanted to know more about the other rider. He'd be his true rival, more so than any scoundrel who won a game of cards.

"Possibly like him, yes." He tightened the knot. "Or some gentleman who can give her the life she wants and deserves." He stepped back. "At any rate, this should hold even the wettest of quilts on a windy day."

"Good job both of you."

John turned to see Fiona stepping off of the porch. "Bill did most of the work."

"Thank you. I do appreciate it." She walked up to the line and tugged. "You're right. Very sturdy. I better go move my sheets if they're not already dry." She smiled at Bill. "I know you've been patient with me on laundry days."

Bill blushed. "Aw, it's not been bad, miss. I'd been meaning to help you with this." He nodded at John. "When he came over asking for posts and a shovel, I had a good idea who'd sent him out."

After a quick glance and slight smile at John, Fiona asked Bill, "So you know about the outhouse?"

John couldn't resist teasing her. "He might have told me I was jumping the gun a little."

Fiona laughed. "I thought you might find out about my trick too soon. Ah well. If you're not doing much else, I could use a hand with folding or hanging sheets."

"This is where I go find other chores besides women's work." Bill tipped his hat and hurried off.

She shook her head. "Silly man. One day he'll want clean anything and there won't be a woman around to help him. He'll wish he'd learned something before then."

"I agree." Plus, Bill's running away left him as alone with Fiona as he could be on a Pony Express station. He held out a hand. "Shall we?"

After a chuckle, she shook her head and walked toward the corral. "Come on, fancy pants. You know where my laundry is."

A little disappointed about not getting to hold her hand, he followed her to the row of drying bedclothes. She knelt to feel the bottommost edges of the first sheet before standing. "This one is dry but you don't really have to help."

He grabbed the end of the draped fabric closest to him. "I don't mind. I'm tall enough to keep the hems from dragging the ground."

"I'd appreciate it." She took the other end before holding it by the two corners and folding.

John mimicked her actions. He knew this dance after having helped his mother often enough. When she took his corners, their fingers brushed. A sliver of desire went from his hands to his heart. He glanced up from where she held the sheet into her rounded eyes and asked her, "A little early in the year for static, don't you think?"

She finished the folding and draped the fabric over the corral. "The day has been especially dry, I suppose." She took the next sheet. "I'll expect this one to not shock us both."

He helped like before and grinned when the same tingle went through him. Touching her caused his heart to race, humidity in the air or not. She didn't meet his gaze afterward or say anything. "We might be glad there's no thunderstorm overhead. Otherwise, we'd be giving lightning back to the sky."

"Probably so. Although, if there were a chance of rain, all this would be in the house and draped all over the kitchen." She took the last nearly folded sheet from him. "Which reminds me I need to set out the cooled pies and start supper for later."

"Definitely women's work, although, I don't mind being a taster as you go," he said and watched as she gathered the stack of sheets. He took them from her. "Open the door for me and I'll help with cooking if you like."

She did as he'd suggested. "Aren't you a gentleman? If you're not careful, I'll ask the Express bosses to transfer you to station help."

The idea almost stopped him cold as he followed her up the steps. He walked into the kitchen in a daze before letting her take the sheets from him.

Fiona didn't look back as she hurried through the room. "Let me put these on the table and we'll get started. I'll be right back."

He nodded and leaned against the counter as she left. He could be switched to a stationary job here, but did he want that? Every time he connected with Fiona, no matter how brief of a touch, he wanted more. Like, more time together, more of a life together, more of a commitment. He put his hands in his pockets to stop their trembling.

No. He stood up and crossed his arms. He wanted to enjoy his youth and not marry too young. Women might be spinsters by the time they were nineteen but men never reached confirmed bachelor until their forties. He had a decade or two yet.

When Fiona walked in, John glanced up at her. "I'm not interested in settling down anytime soon."

"Hello to you, too, and who asked you to do such a silly thing?" She shook her head and held her hands up before letting them fall. "Never mind. I don't want to entertain crazy ideas when I have things to do."

"You were talking about my staying here for good to help you. I won't. I like being free and riding fast, not folding sheets and stringing clothesline everywhere."

"Fine, then. Don't stay." She grabbed a paring knife from a canning jar used as a utensil holder. "I can cut my own vegetables and haul my own water with no help from you, too. Just in case those were the next two chores you were wanting to protest as well."

Shame filled him. He'd been projecting his own fears and reasons onto her. She'd just wanted a little help around there and he'd blown everything out of proportion. "Sorry, I mean I do want to help you today, but also to keep going on mail runs. One pays better than the other."

She continued to set out vegetables with her back to him. "I completely understand. You're free to go at any time."

"All right. I'd like to stay, though, until the next trip east." He shuffled from one foot to the other while waiting for her response. She began slicing the yellow squash. Feeling a bit useless, he asked, "Can I help cut something?"

"You can, and here." She handed him the small knife she was using handle first. "Take this and peel potatoes for me."

John took the knife and picked up a potato. Fiona was biting her lip and he couldn't help but wonder why. "Will do." After a long silence, he said, "I don't hate the idea of being with you, just so you know." He watched as her shoulders relaxed and almost sighed in relief as the tension lifted from the air.

She gave him a wary glance. "That's good? I don't hate being here with you, either. Although, I'd like it if you left a lot less potato on the skin."

"Oh, yeah." He refocused on his peeling. "I mean, when I decide on what to do with my life, I want a good nest egg built up. The Express isn't going to last forever and I need to make the most of the higher wages."

Fiona placed three more potatoes and all of the tomatoes in front of him. "These, too, if you don't mind, and slice all of them somewhat thin." She began cutting the peeled potato into bite sized pieces. "I know what you mean about nothing lasting forever. Mason and I could go by rail only so far. One day soon, the trains will run from one coast to the other."

"That's exactly what I thought. Why put riders in danger for slower mail delivery when there are trains to do the job better?"

She glanced up at him. "So, I suppose you'll need plans before you decide to plan."

He laughed at her wry grin. She had a point. He'd need to line up another job before the Pony Express well ran dry. "Reckon I will. Know any new store that might be hiring?"

"A couple, if Randall and I have our way."

The other man's name settled on him like a cold and very wet blanket. Something stuck in his craw about her being anywhere near the man and he didn't know why. He could see himself settling down in several years with Fiona. Years, though, and not soon just to keep Randall from sweeping her away. "Two, huh? Opening a shop with a man does seem like something a woman would do with her husband. I didn't know you were so serious about him."

"I'm not." She put the diced vegetables into a smaller bowl. "Thus, the two shops for two people. We may not even end up in the same part of the country."

"He seems awfully sweet on you." John picked up the tail end slice of a tomato and ate it. He liked that she wasn't in a hurry to find a man. She never indicated she was, he had to admit, but still. A man couldn't expect any woman to wait for him when so many other good men were available. "He's almost as sweet as this tomato is."

She frowned and paused in slicing up an onion. "Sweet? Let me taste."

He picked up another tail end. Her hands were busy so he held up the slice for her to bite into. When she leaned forward for the taste, her lips brushed his fingertips. The electricity wasn't static, but managed to make his nerve endings tingle. Desire rushed through him and he took her upper arms. She dropped her knife and onion and her eyes widened, their bright green luring him in closer. "You're such a beauty," he said, and then kissed her.

John wrapped his arms around her. She nestled into him and he groaned against her mouth. Every inch of his skin longed to be next to hers. Dimly aware of others being able to walk in on them, he tried to pull away. She broke off the kiss with a slight smack before kissing him again, captivating him completely. He needed her, in his arms, in his bed, and in his life.

After a hum, she broke off their kiss again and stepped back. "My goodness. I need to grow more tomatoes, don't I?"

"I…" John was still lost in her touch. When Fiona left his arms completely, he saw her hands were still damp from cutting vegetables. He began to say something about how the next time they kissed to make sure she had clean hands but he stopped himself. If one kiss could lead to him thinking about forever with her, what would two kisses do?

He didn't want to find out. Not yet, and not until after the Pony Express stopped running. She hadn't waited for him to add anything more. Instead, she was rebuilding the stove's fire and putting out pans for cooking. She seemed unaffected until he caught her hand shaking as she dumped vegetables from one bowl into a cookpot.

She tapped the near empty bowl to dislodge a couple of clingy potato chunks. "So, I can handle the rest of this myself if you have other things you need to do this afternoon." She smiled at him. "You're a fun distraction but I do need to get dinner ready for the boys."

Her lack of a response took him aback. Had she not felt the air crackle with electricity as he had? "We don't need to talk about what just happened?"

"No. I don't think we do." She looked past him to the back door. "Hello there." She took a step away from John. "I didn't hear you come in."

After turning to find Mason standing there, John nodded and said, "Hello."

"You two are as jumpy as cats in a rocking chair factory. Is anything wrong?"

Fiona shook her head and smiled before saying, "No. Not at all."

CHAPTER SEVEN

Fiona took a step away from John to give credence to her next denial. "We were gossiping, shame to say." She needed to distract Mason by putting the focus on anything but what he might have seen in the room. "Never mind all that. How was your run?"

"Not too bad." Her brother went over to the vegetables lined up on the counter and picked up a carrot. "Signs of natives everywhere but I didn't see anyone." He took a bite of the carrot, chewing it while he said, "I suppose they were blending into the land too well."

"Goodness, Mace." She slapped him on the arm with the wooden spoon. "Have some manners, would you?"

He laughed and took another bite. "Manner don't matter out here, do they, John?"

"Nope."

She glared at John and his mischievous grin. "He's talking with food in his mouth and you're egging him on? Out, both of you, and take one of the pies with you for lunch. I've got work to do and you two are bothering me."

"Oh, she's riled up now." Mason took one of the

small fried pies and tilted his head toward the dining room. "Let's go and let this hen settle down a bit."

Fiona put her hands on her hips. "Nothing's wrong and I'm not in a mood bad enough to run you off." Her voice sounded too loud, even to her. She shook her head as Mason laughed. "Fine, go on with you both. I'm far too busy to humor the likes of you."

John had the nerve to wink at her before he scooped up a vegetable pie and disappeared with his food, too. As soon as he was out of sight, she smiled at his cheekiness. She went back to chopping up the last few vegetables for dinner. The knife faltered while she cut up the last carrot for tonight's stew. Despite her best efforts, she couldn't ignore the memory of John's lips against hers.

Randall had never been so bold and more than a small part of her liked John's audacity.

If only he were less interested in gaming and gambling away his earnings, she'd be able to allow herself to develop feelings for him. After dusting her hands off on her apron, she placed the pot of root vegetables on the stove. The rest of the morning's fresh water went in, too.

With the empty bucket in hand, she went to the door as a horn sounded in the distance. The sound reminded her how the beds needed to be made. More so if the rider had come from far enough to need sleep. She set the pail aside for later to focus on other tasks.

The clean sheets still lay stacked on the dining room table. Fiona scooped them up and hurried through to the bedrooms. So far, none of the riders were fussy about neatness. Still, she liked to make the beds nice for them and to keep the surfaces dusted. The floors needed sweeping but she'd have to do that after dinner. Soon, she finished making the last bed and went into the hallway.

An express rider she'd seen a time or two before came up to her, hat in hand. "Good afternoon. Is what's cooking for anyone?"

"Not yet, I'm afraid. There's vegetable pies for now, though, and for cold meals later." She returned his smile. "Come along then, and I'll show you."

"Thank you, ma'am."

The young man was polite like most of the riders were. She felt sure there had to be some bad apples in the mix but she hadn't met one yet. When they reached the kitchen, she pointed at the plate where the vegetable pies lay under a cloth. "Help yourself while I get your water."

"I can get it myself."

"No need to do so when I'm headed there anyway. Make yourself comfortable, and thank you for the offer." She grabbed the pail and headed outside. When the wind blew just right, sun-warmed sage perfumed the air as they walked to the water pump. After a couple of pumps of the handle, she had a full pail.

Fiona lingered a little, watching the water bugs dance on the surface of the horses' trough. She glanced up and looked around. Other than the usual birdsong, the place seemed oddly quiet. Livestock made a slight noise but not much. The sky seemed endless and almost too blue to bear. She enjoyed the quiet for a couple minutes more before taking the water into the kitchen.

Once in the house, laughter and loud talking in the

dining room made up for the peace outside. The ruckus from Express riders always made her glad Mason had been her only brother. Thinking they might be thirsty, she poured several glasses of the cool water and carried three held together into the dining room.

Bill, the station keeper, sat with John and four other riders as they played cards. A stack of peanuts sat in front of each player with a huge bunch in the middle of the table. She tried to smile. "Does anyone want something to drink?" They all looked at her at the same time, talking over each other in their rush to answer. She set three of the glasses down and went for more. As she served the remaining three, she ignored John as much as he ignored her. She glanced at him only when certain he couldn't see her do so. His laughing and joking around with cards in his hands didn't bother her. Not at all. If he wanted to waste his life on games of chance, so be it. He might be fun to steal kisses from, but nothing else.

Fiona slipped back into the kitchen and stirred the stew. The vegetables needed a little more cooking to be tender. She wanted to use the time wisely by catching up on her sewing, so she went to her tiny room to retrieve her sewing bag before sitting in the parlor. Only one of the parlor chairs had cushions so she dragged the seat to the window for more of the late afternoon light.

A few minutes into her work, trying to focus, she heard footsteps on the wooden floor. After someone cleared his throat, she glanced up to see Bill standing there. "Did you need something mended? If you do, I'd be glad to add it to my work."

"Naw." He pulled up a smooth wooden chair

across from her. "I thought I'd come in here and wait for dinner with you."

She couldn't help but smile at the slight hint. "I'm hungry, too. The potatoes weren't as tender as I'd like. As soon as I finish affixing this button, the food should be ready."

"Good." The chair creaked as he shifted his weight around. "Tomorrow's supplies day."

"I have a list ready for you."

"Thank you." She tied a knot in the thread and put the needle in her pincushion. "Now, let's see if I can set the table around the riders' card game."

Bill stood when Fiona did and followed her into the dining room. He said, "Wrap it up, fellas. Grub is ready."

She went on into the kitchen and left their groaning behind her. After giving the stew another stir, she took the trivet and a stack of bowls for the table where peanut shells littered the surface, but she didn't react. John wasn't in the room and she wanted to ask why but needed to get the dinner to them first.

Fiona went back to the kitchen, grabbed pot holders, and carried the food for them into the room. "It's hot, so wait until I bring utensils for you." They barely paid attention to her warning. She hurried, grabbing a ladle, spoons, and a basket of yesterday's bread.

Once she went back into the kitchen to have her own meal, she realized she'd forgotten to fill for her, too. John hadn't come in and there might be barely enough for him. She glanced at the dishcloth covering the vegetable pies on the counter. She could have a cold meal and didn't mind doing so on a warm and busy day. Several were left since she'd made enough to share with hungry riders too busy to stop for a proper meal. She wrapped up three for others and saved one for her dinner.

She wrapped her pie up in its own napkin to catch the crumbs. While eating, the mess of the peanut shells the boys had just left in the dining room still bothered her. She'd have to sweep the litter up after they were finished. Their boots would track the shells everywhere, too. She sighed before taking another bite. Running the domestic side of a station was constant work. No sooner she'd finish one task, another four popped up for her. She took another bite and figured she had a solution to prevent future messes. The next time the boys bet for peanuts, she'd set a bowl for their shells on the table with a stern warning. Just as she took a last bite, John walked into the room.

"Is the soup that bad?"

Fiona chewed fast and swallowed. "No. I forgot to get myself some stew, so I decided to have leftover pie instead." She watched as he retrieved a bowl and spoon for himself. "You'll have to tell me if dinner is any good."

"Will do."

He wandered out and she dipped a cup of water from the pail. Before she could take a drink, he came back in with a full bowl of soup and leaned against the counter next to her. "Some time, we should try sitting down to a meal together."

"I could bring two chairs in here for us, or me, since you'll be off on a run most of the time."

John nodded while stirring his food. "Or we could eat with the others."

She'd wanted to have her meals in the dining room but Mason had convinced her that familiarity with the men would lead to liberties she wouldn't want. She had to admit he was right; an inch given often led to a mile taken.

"The meal is very good." He dipped a chunk of bread into the broth. "I scooped out the last bowlful and hope you make more next time."

"Thank you, I will. I credit my help this afternoon."

"I'd have to disagree. It's all your ability."

Her face warmed from the flattery. "I'm just happy no one is left hungry." Wanting to stop him from embarrassing her with more praise, she asked, "How was your game tonight? I saw you left early."

John chuckled and gave her an embarrassed smile. "Yeah, no sense in staying around after I'd lost my last peanut."

Dread settled onto her like a stack of books pressing down on her chest. Today they played for trivial things but what about next time? Would they up the bets until real money was won and lost? She shook her head. "Or the stakes might get higher the longer you sit at the table?"

He grinned and ate the last bite. "Yeah, I'd have to move up to walnuts, but I don't have any." He put his bowl and spoon in the wash tub. "Never mind cashews or pecans."

She tried to smile at his making light of gambling. She didn't want to see him follow her father's path, but his business was none of her concern. Except, their kiss had left her wanting more from life and especially from him. Folding her napkin into a small square, she couldn't look at him while she asked, "So, have you ever bet with anything besides peanuts?" She glanced up into his eyes. "With something that meant a lot to you?"

A pained look swept his face before he frowned and shrugged. "No, not really. I have a rule to never bet anything I couldn't stand to lose."

***

He'd lied to her. A huge, fat, no take backs falsehood. Someone, some young man named Hyatt, had come in with a stack of bowls. John took the welcome interruption to thank her for dinner again and go for an evening walk. Leaning against one of the few trees lining the creek, he sighed. Fiona may not mean everything to him, yet, but was fast taking over his every thought. If she ever found out he'd gambled for her affections, she'd never speak to him again.

He couldn't blame her. While he didn't know what having a father was like, if his mother had lost everything due to bad behavior, he'd be sore, too. Fiona was wrong to have a burr under her saddle about his gaming; he wouldn't bet anything he couldn't afford to lose. Only, he'd bet and lost on courting her.

John walked down to the creek while watching the sunset fill the sky with color.

He'd thought he held a winning hand. Heck, in any other game, a straight flush took it all. He wanted to run up to the station and tell Fiona what had happened at Cold Springs station. How he'd gambled and lost, but wouldn't play again.

Between her addicting kisses and losing to Rob, John couldn't find joy in betting anymore. He shook his head as the orange sky above him faded to dark reds.

A smart woman would set her cap for Randall and be done with it. She'd have slapped John for his boldness the moment their lips touched.

The twilight faded into darkness as a new rider arrived and another one left. He turned to go back to the station, determined to make plans and ride off for a new home station. He didn't need to see Fiona and Randall create a romance from their friendship.

John stepped up to the back door and heard Rob, the man he'd lost Fiona to, before seeing him. He paused before opening the door. Fiona was laughing at whatever Rob had said. He didn't care why he'd rather see her with Randall than Rob. All he knew was the man had better keep his hands off of her.

He walked in and found Rob sitting on the counter while Fiona cleaned the stove. Forcing a smile for a congeniality he didn't feel, he said, "Hello, Fiona. Lambert.

Fiona stopped cleaning and smiled back at John. "There you are. I thought you might have left with the last mochila."

Rob grinned. "Williamson. Good to see you again."

John gritted his teeth. "Likewise."

She looked from one man to the other. "You've met, then?"

"We have," Rob said. "He rides up to Cold Springs from here and I come in from Fish Springs."

She smiled. "That's a lot of springs, don't you think?"

"Don't be fooled by their grand names," Rob told her. "Most of them are muddy spots on the ground where water tries to reach the surface."

She leaned toward him, resting a hand on the

countertop. "We crossed the desert on the train but never stopped long enough to look at anything in length."

"You traveled with someone?" Rob asked and continued before she could answer, "I hope a sister or two for John's sake. He could use a girl almost as pretty as you to come home to."

Fiona laughed. "You do have a silver tongue. No, my brother and I came here from the east."

"Why do I think you mean east of the Atlantic?" Rob put his hand on the counter in a mirror of hers.

"Because it's true. We came here from Ireland to create a new life." She glanced at John. "I'd like to work hard, save up, and find my fortune."

She seemed to be speaking to John's heart with her last sentence. He'd always dreamed of being free and rushing out to grab life on his own terms. As he watched her talk with Rob, he wondered if having her come along on his adventures as his partner was possible. Would she even want to go with him and leave her brother behind?

"Sounds like you have a perfect plan," Rob said. "Try to remember us lesser people when you're a wealthy woman."

She chuckled and shook her head. "I don't know about wealthy, but I would like enough to pay my bills and tuck some into savings."

"You do sound like the perfect woman," Rob quipped and grinned at John. "Makes me glad I decided to come as far as Carson City for myself."

Each glance the Cold Creek rider gave Fiona irritated John. Something about the other man spurred him to win at any cost. He hated every laugh she rewarded Rob with. In an effort to break up the festivities between the two, he picked up the empty cook pot. "I can help you wash up if you like."

Rob's eyebrows rose and he looked at Fiona. "Don't tell me you have him trained for women's work."

She chuckled. "I didn't have to. John is just a naturally kind and helpful man."

"Well, he's not the only one in the country." Rob took the pot from John. "Lead the way, fair lady, and let me help you wash up before it gets too late."

John stood between them and the back door. "It was my idea. And anyway, don't you have something else to do, like take a bath or wash your clothes?"

"Nope. I'm as clean as anyone else here." Rob looked him up and down. "Maybe cleaner." He turned to Fiona. "Come on. Let's get these washed and you tell me all about how you came to Carson City."

She smiled at him. "Very well. You can help tonight since John's helped me so much today." Her smile faded as she looked at John. "Besides, don't you have a card game waiting for you?"

"You heard the lady, Williamson." He opened the door for her while giving John a smug look. "You're not on kitchen duty tonight."

Rob led her outside, talking too low for him to hear. John frowned at how smoothly the other man had whisked her away. "Damn it," he muttered and turned on his heel to walk to the front of the station.

Several of the riders sat around on the porch railing and on benches. John spotted Mason on his left with an open space next to him. He returned others' greetings and ambled over to Fiona's brother. "Hey."

"So, my sister run you out of her kitchen?"

"No. More like some yahoo is taking over her attentions."

Mason chuckled. "That's what you and the yahoo think. Fiona is firmly in charge of her affections, not you or him."

John glanced around them but the others were too caught up in their own stories to pay him any mind. He wasn't fond of the boys ribbing him in front of Fiona. "I know she's her own woman. I'm not trying to push her either way."

"Uh huh."

Mason didn't seem to believe him so John doubled down. "Not that I wouldn't want to push her a little toward me. She's a pretty gal, no doubt about it. She's a great cook and I like how she has this no-nonsense air about her. She'll go far once her shop opens."

"Yeah, Fee's been after opening a store since we were children. She'd line up rocks and flowers for display and make me pretend to buy them from her. I wanted to play horses and farmer so I'd come in and buy flowers for my animals to eat."

John could imagine them as youngsters. "She'd probably make a good mother to her own children."

"Maybe. I wouldn't mind being an uncle to a rascal or two of hers." He grinned at John. "Especially if they turn out all nice and quiet like her."

"Somehow, I think you're kidding me about that."

"Ah, boyo, it's called an Irish temper for a reason." He nodded to their right as Rob and Fiona walked up to the front porch. "I'll bet he'd turn tail at the first sign of her bad side." He nudged John. "I know I always do."

John frowned when seeing the couple arm in arm. "Hope it's easy to keep her happy."

"It is. No gambling or lying and she's fine."

Fiona didn't acknowledge him as she went up the stairs to the front door. The others lowered their voices while Rob opened the door for her and she let go of Rob's arm. "You didn't have to walk me to the front door. I'm quite safe with so many men here."

"You probably are, miss, but you never know what ruffians might be around." He turned to John. "Right, Williamson?"

"I'm looking at one right now," he replied.

Rob laughed. "He's a funny man," he quipped before opening the door for her. "Let's go inside and I'll let you show me to my room."

"All right."

They disappeared inside and John couldn't help but stare after them. He wanted to go, pull the two apart and tell her he had feelings for her. Only, his gambling for her and the lying by omission kept him in his seat. She might not know now, but Rob could be counted on to tell her everything about the bet at Cold Springs. She'd be furious and hurt but the only thing Rob would care about was winning. "He doesn't deserve her," he said to Mason.

"You're sounding awfully jealous right now. As if you don't like Fee being pawed over by the new guy. I always wanted a brother. Wonder if they'll get married?"

Every word felt like a knife digging deeper into his chest and John growled, "Go to hell."

"Naw, you're already there, and I'm in no hurry to join you."

CHAPTER EIGHT

The next morning, John stalled in going to the breakfast table. He'd missed the middle of the night run, which was fine. He wanted to see Fiona once more, anyway. The only problem was if Rob hadn't been the rider who left last night. He didn't want to face his smug face just yet.

As soon as his shirt was tucked and buttoned, John left the room for something to eat. The house was mostly silent. He'd have a quick bite to eat and wait outside for the upcoming horse. The express boy probably wasn't expecting to stop and he tried to care but couldn't. He needed some space between him and Fiona, or actually between him and Rob.

The floors creaked under his feet and as soon as he stepped into the kitchen, he regretted it. Fiona was there, thankfully alone, kneading dough. A smudge of flour graced her nose.

She glanced over at him. "Good morning, stranger. You're all Mr. Helpful one day and gone the next. Are you feeling well?"

Her smile lured him closer. "'Morning to you, too.

Well, I reckon you had someone else helping you last night. No room left for me."

Her eyebrows rose as she resumed kneading the dough. "Rob did seem a little clingy, didn't he?" She shook her head. "He's a fine man and full of interesting stories, but that's no reason for you to run off." She looked past John to the doorway. "And speak of the devil. Good morning."

Rob strolled over to her. "Me? No, I'm an angel." He winked. "Just ask my momma when you meet her."

Fiona laughed. "Even the worst boys are good to their mother." She plopped the dough into a bowl and covered it with a cloth. "So try again, pony boy."

John narrowed his eyes at Rob. Rob and Fiona were far too familiar with each other. Had he kissed Fiona or even tried to? Just the thought made John want to punch him. The air seemed too hot and unbearable all of a sudden. He shifted his weight from one foot to the other as the other two talked. When the conversation hit a pause, John said, "I'll be going as soon as the next mail run is here."

"Oh?" Rob replied. "Sorry. I forgot you were here."

She smacked him with a spare hand towel. "For shame. Be nice to him." She turned to John. "You've not had breakfast. Take one of my cold meals for later when you're able to slow enough to eat."

Without waiting for an answer, she began throwing various dry meats, wrapped cheese, and biscuits into a handkerchief. Her speed impressed him as she tied up the corners and held the food out to him. "Go on and do be careful. Rob says the natives back east are getting..." she glanced at Rob. "Riled?" He nodded and she turned to John. "Riled up."

"Thank you, Fee. I'll keep an eye out for trouble." He nodded at Rob. "Lambert."

Rob just grinned and put his arm around Fiona. "Take your time and do be careful."

John looked from one to the other before walking out. The cold morning air made him want to turn around and head for the warm bed he'd left. But, that would mean passing those two again, and no thank you.

Instead, he sat on the porch. The next rider would be along any minute. Might as well get comfortable and think about the future plans he didn't want to make. He didn't want to marry anyone and be tied down to one place too soon. No falling in love just because a beautiful woman had the sweetest lips he'd ever kissed. If a man were to stop to court every woman who could make a stew better than his momma, men would be lined up and circling the station.

A horn sounded in the distance, signaling an approaching rider. John stood and Bill came out of the barn with a horse saddled and ready to go. He nodded at the older man. "Morning."

"G'morning." He led the horse to the gate before throwing the reins over the animal's head. "You heard about the trouble to the east?"

"Yeah, something like that."

"All right. Ride fast and don't take crazy chances."

The approaching of horse hooves grew louder. "Will do," John replied.

The new rider skidded to a stop and hopped off. While bill changed the mochila from one horse to the other, the rider said, "I'm stopping here for a while?"

"If you don't mind."

"Naw. I've been going most of the night. I could use something to eat, too."

John hopped up onto the fresh horse. "The cook is one of the best around." Before either man could reply, he nudged the animal's flank and they took off. He rode into the sunrise. The Carson River flowed beside him and the horse seemed as ready to go as John was. The golden light flooded the basin as the sun climbed higher. The men and fresh horses were ready for him at every station.

The ride between the first two stations gave him too much time to think about life. The easy and flat road didn't help. He'd prefer nothing coming at him while he went, either physically or emotionally, but Fiona had changed him.

A man shouldn't be giving up his freedom for two stinkin' kisses, he thought. Yet, even thinking about her doing the same with Rob, never mind going on and imagining it, made him sick. He might not have won the card game for her, yet, when she looked at him and smiled, he felt like he'd won everything good in the world.

Fort Churchill was up next. He always liked taking his time under the shade tree or two before moving on. He grinned. Of course, his slowing down was most other people's too fast. Stopping before reaching the station was always best, too, because the fresh horse stomped and paced too much for John to enjoy his meal.

He eased the horse into a slow gallop. At first, he struggled a bit with retrieving his apple from Fiona's handkerchief in his shoulder bag. The canteen was easier but the water was stale. He hadn't thought to refill it while at Carson City. He took another bite and knew why; Fiona had kept him distracted and off his game.

The apple half eaten, he stopped at the new horse and station hand waiting for him. "Give me a few seconds," he said, and gave his animal the rest of his apple. By the time the snack was eaten, the mochila rested on the new saddle. He hopped on and took off for the next stop.

He'd expected to see the station by now. With its location at the base of a low hill, anyone riding in from the west would have seen the hint of a building or two by now. As John approached, he soon discovered why there wasn't a station there anymore. A heavy smell of charred wood still clung to the burned wood where the station had been. A couple of fresh graves lay to the far side. Both had mounds of rocks heaped over them to keep the wolves away. He knelt his head for a moment to offer a silent prayer for those who'd died. When he was done, he nudged his horse's flanks before resuming the run to let the men at Desert Station know about the attack at Hooten Wells. He figured it made good sense to not loiter when there were enemies behind every hill.

After several miles, both man and animal were exhausted, and he wanted to slow down to finish the last of his food. A long drink of anything might be nice, too. His canteen was empty and the next station was several miles away. Unwilling to wait until the next stop, he reached back into his shoulder bag and rummaged for whatever was left of Fiona's cooking. A biscuit or a few bites of cheese might tame his hunger for a while.

When he'd eaten last, he'd retied the knots too tight so he pulled the bag around to better reach them. Trusting the horse knew the way, John fiddled with the handkerchief for a few seconds before retrieving the biscuit. The late afternoon sun still shone hot and he'd want a drink after this.

Before John could take a bite, the horse stumbled at a dip in the road. The sudden drop before the animal's sudden stop sent him flying over the horse's neck and to the ground. His head hit the ground with a crunch and knocked the sense out of him.

By the time he could lift his chin and look around, the horse was small and off in the distance. He'd continued on as if a rider still guided him. John shook his head to clear it and grimaced from the pain. At least the mail continued, he thought before his world went gray.

***

Something tickled his nose. John swiped at the tickle before waking with a start. Stars shown overhead. He struggled to sit up and remembered what had happened. He rubbed his eyes free of the dust and felt where his forehead had scraped the ground. Every part of him ached.

He scanned the horizon but saw nothing resembling a campfire anywhere. A stagecoach or another rider should have come through by now. Something disruptive must have happened nearby. He looked east, then west, and saw nothing but vague shapes illuminated by starlight. There'd been mention of the route moving north where the road was safer.

No one had said anything to him, but then he hadn't been paying attention to anything but Fiona.

John rose to his knees before standing. He still had his bag and canteen, not that either did him any good. Desert Station should be to the east of him. While he wanted to go back to Carson City, the distance and lack of water made up his mind for him. The lack of campfires might mean the lack of hostiles ready to kill him. All he could do was start walking.

CHAPTER NINE

Riders came and went at Carson City. Fiona tried to keep up with who was named what but there were so many of them. Just as she'd learn a rider's name and get to know him, he'd find another station house to be his base home. Other than Mason, Randall, and their station keeper, Bill, John was the first who lingered in her mind long after he'd left.

Two weeks passed with each day being the same. Recent Indian attacks back east had everyone on edge. She tensed every time a rider approached but it was never John. Her brother hadn't heard anything about where John might be, but his run usually ran west rather than east where John had gone on his last run. Whenever Rob rode by, he'd done just that, rode by without saying anything to her or even Bill. Even Randall was too busy to do much more than say hello, grab a bite to eat, and ride on after giving her a hug.

She straightened from her crouch by the pea plants. This afternoon's westbound mail was due any minute and she wanted to be there when the rider changed horses. Chances were, he'd have news about something so she'd know one way or another about

John.

After making sure the bottom of her apron was gathered enough to keep the pea pods from spilling, she hurried to the corral. Bill stood there with the fresh horse. "Do you think he'll know something?"

"Maybe. I hope so. John's a decent young man."

Fiona glanced at him. His worried tone matched the worry in her heart. She ignored how fear of something horrible happening left her breathless. Instead, she focused on the approaching rider. The way he moved reminded her of Rob and, sure enough, as he approached them, she realized he wasn't John after all.

A pony boy staggered down the steps while yawning. "I reckon I can take the next run. Can't sleep around here, anyway. They're up to a fuss on the front porch."

She nodded. "I'm sorry. It's been such a warm day and they forget not everyone rides all day."

"Yeah. S'kay." He moved his shoulder bag to his back in preparation. "I forget, too, unless I'm running all night."

Fiona watched as Rob rushed up before pulling the horse to a hard stop. He jumped down. Bill moved the mochila from one animal to another in one fluid motion. She returned Rob's smile as the other rider headed off west. "Hello, nice to see you again."

Rob pulled her into a loose hug. "You're always a sight for sore eyes. I'd rather see you than a passel of sage brush any day."

"Thank you, I think?" She returned his grin while stepping out of his embrace. "I enjoy being more attractive than the local shrubbery."

"You are." He held out his arm for her. "What's new around here? Anything worth telling?"

She switched hands, holding her bunched up apron in her other hand before taking his arm. They walked toward the stationhouse. "Not much at all. Another day, another round of riders, meals, and cleaning." She nodded at her vegetables. "With a little gardening thrown in, of course."

"Of course."

"I've been wondering, have you heard anything from John Williamson? He's not been by in several days. All of the trouble with natives lately has me worried for him."

"You hadn't heard?"

The bottom seemed to fall out of her stomach. So the worst had happened and she'd not known at all. Fiona didn't want to ask, didn't want to truly know the answer, but couldn't help herself. "Was he killed?"

"No, not yet," he said while holding open the kitchen door for her.

She glanced at him. He had an amused expression on his face and she wanted to shove him like she'd do to Mason when he was mean. Yet, she couldn't help the relief filling her and overriding any anger from his horrible teasing. Her eyes stung with building tears and she sniffed. "Oh thank God. With the new fort, additional troops being called for, and stations attacked, I'd been concerned."

Rob stared at Fiona before taking her by the shoulders. "Hey, no need to cry. He'll be fine in a couple of days or so, maybe sooner if he's allowed to ride."

"What happened? Is he truly fine or hurt worse

than you'll admit?" She dumped the pea pods on the counter and wiped her damp cheeks.

"He was thrown somewhere west of Desert Station. Fortunately, he hit his head."

She glared at him. A brain injury wasn't a good outcome at all. "I don't see how that can be remotely fortunate."

"You're right. Just because he's a stubborn cuss doesn't mean his skull can't be cracked." Rob leaned against the counter. "He was knocked out for a while, he says, but found his way to a nearby stop. The station keeper made him stay a few days."

"It's been longer than that now."

"He's been going out on short runs but couldn't take so much movement. I'd seen a few times where he collapsed after even a trip to a close station and back."

She turned her back to Rob but couldn't help crying over what John must have endured. Her eyes filled with tears again as she tried not to sob out loud.

"Fiona?" He put his arms around her from behind. "I didn't know you cared about him so much."

"I've tried not to. We want different things in life but my heart doesn't listen to me," she said. Rob let go of her and she turned to face him. "If I'd known about his accident, I'd have found a way to him long before now."

He smoothed a stray lock of hair from her forehead. "I have to admit I'm jealous of the guy. I might have won the game but he's the real winner."

A trace of foreboding slithered down her spine. "Game?"

"Yeah. He thought he'd won the right to court you

with a straight flush. If I hadn't held a royal flush, he'd probably be here right now and I'd be back at Desert, nursing an aching head."

Her stomach flip-flopped in her. "You two gambled for me?" He'd played cards and worse, he'd bet for her affections. Here she'd poured her heart out to him about Da, and John had gone ahead to wager for her.

"Just once. It started out as fun. I didn't know he'd be so serious about winning or that I'd be as happy as I am."

Fiona picked up a knife and a potato. "You shouldn't be," she said. Rob couldn't be blamed too much. He didn't know her history. But John did and he broke her heart without even saying a word to her. Rob deserved to know why she was furious, yet, she couldn't bear to be honest with another man only to have him turn around and do the very thing she hated. John's doing so was enough for right now. She shook her head. "Neither one of you truly won because I think you're both losers." Turning to the counter, she began peeling. "In fact, I suggest you find something else to do right now. Please."

"You're angry?" he asked and when she glared at him, he took a step back. "You are. All right, I think they need me outside."

As soon as he'd hurried off, Fiona put down the knife and vegetable before putting her face in her hands. Here she'd been terrified some tribe had tortured John to death while he'd been betting with other riders on their relationship. First, he'd gamble away their love and next would be their livelihoods.

No. She knew this song too well. Her children

wouldn't need to find a new home across an ocean. Not because of her or who she loved.

As she continued with dinner preparations, fury helped her slice up for dinner in record time. A cleaned chicken helped dispel her anger, too. By the time she'd swept the entire house and set the table, the meal was ready.

Fiona put the fried chicken on a plate. A rider had come and gone, yet no one had wandered by to ask when the food might be ready. She shook her head. Rob must have warned everyone to avoid the house until she cooled down. He was a wise man despite his gambling.

She brought the meat into the dining room. After setting down the plate, she glanced up. "John?" He grinned and she couldn't help but smiled back. "You don't look worse for wear."

He walked up to her. "I'm a lot better now."

She smoothed away his hair to examine the scrape on his forehead. "Does it still hurt?"

"Not as bad as it looked. For a while there, I'd see stars even in the daytime." He held her shoulders. "Now I only see them in your eyes."

His sweet words meant nothing now. "Ah, you're not going to tell me about how you'd use a spade on every clover field to find diamonds and win my heart?" She frowned at his confused expression. "What? You seem a little flushed right now. Too bad you're not a prince because I only let royal flushes court me." The color drained from his face. "Yes, I know you played a card game for me. What do you have to say for yourself?"

"I know you don't like gambling because of what

you lost. I didn't like or help you because of any bet."
He put a hand on her arm. "I did those things because
I care for you."

Fiona shrugged off his touch and escaped into the
kitchen. She cared for him, too, but after what he'd
done? She couldn't let herself fall for him any more
than she already had. When he walked in, she gave him
a bowl of vegetables. "Here, take these out to the
dining room and call the others."

John took the bowl but hesitated, shifting his
weight from one foot to the other as he asked,
"You...love me, don't you?"

She couldn't face him. He'd said love? Did she?
Maybe before Rob told her about the game. And now?
Could she love him? She grabbed the potatoes and
butter dish before turning to face him. "No. I don't
even like you."

CHAPTER TEN

John watched as Fiona brought in more bread. The other men were still chatty but quieted down every time she walked into the room. Rob had probably blabbed to everyone and John couldn't blame him.

She disappeared into the kitchen once more and the conversation volume increased. One of the riders said, "Sore at y'all or not, that little gal is the best cook this side of the Mississippi."

"Who's the best on the east side?"

"My momma."

He tried to smile while the others laughed. They talked all around him but he couldn't listen. Not when she was in the next room with his heart. He needed to fix things between him and her.

He pushed his plate to the middle of the table. "Here. I'm not hungry." The pony boys and station keeper fell silent as he stood and went to the kitchen.

Fiona sat on the counter while eating her dinner. Her spoon stopped halfway to her mouth before she put it and her plate down. "Yes?" She hopped off of the counter. "Did you need something?"

"I need you to not be angry with me anymore." John walked up to her and quietly added, "I did a stupid thing, gambling for you, and promise it'll never happen again."

She put her food down and crossed her arms. "I see. Your gesture is very noble, but useless. Gamble as much as you'd like. Bet the entire world and everything in it. I don't care."

A foolish man might cheer at being given permission to gamble but John didn't quite trust her sincerity. "What if I never bet on anything again? If I said I loved you enough to spend the rest of my life with you even if we both live to be a hundred or so?"

"Your words sound pretty. I want to believe them."

"But you heard the same from your father."

She nodded, hugging her arms tighter. "Every time."

He wanted to break through, hold her and reassure her about how he wouldn't slide back into bad habits. "Fiona, I don't need the cards or the games. I'm just having fun and killing time until the next horse needs a rider. I don't do it because I'm desperate or need another coin for a drink."

"I think you should go." She turned her back to him and picked up her plate. "Dinner is nearly over and I have work to do," she said while scraping her dish into the scraps bucket.

John couldn't leave her. Not like this and not without trying just one more time to convince her he was sorry. "What if I helped you with chores?"

"No, I'm able to do everything myself. I think the boys are more fun than I'll be." She pointed toward the door. "Go on so I can get started."

Leaving the room on his own kept her from throwing him out any more forcefully. He headed for the back door to avoid the others and headed for the water pump. Warmth rose up from the ground as he walked, warming the cooling desert evening. He sat on the trough's edge and trailed his fingertips along the water surface, breaking up the dancing moonlight.

She hadn't said she loved him.

When he'd walked in earlier, finding her busy and focused until she noticed him too, her smile brightened everything around them. After a quick shake of his head, he smacked water from the trough. He'd ruined everything with one silly game, but he'd meant what he said about never gambling again.

What did people do when they couldn't play games, though? There had to be more to life than working, eating, and sleeping. He snorted a laugh. Well, there was bedding and not sleeping. Fun, sure, but not a game.

John stood. His head ached almost as much as his heart. The day had ended up opposite from what he'd planned and now he needed to rework everything in Fiona's favor. He'd get some healing sleep before starting fresh in the morning when he planned on being so damn charming, she'd believe him and fall into his arms forever. Even better, he'd ask Mason for help. Her brother knew her the best; she'd forgive him if Mason forgave him first.

He grinned and headed back to the house. He'd give Fiona a break from him for now, make his plans, and win her back without any game needed.

***

Fiona couldn't help but grin when spotting the

Sacramento newspaper in among the parlor room clutter. Sometimes the men's mess was a blessing. She scooped up the items, put them where they belonged, and kept the paper to read the classifieds.

The house was as quiet as a place could be; the more exhausted men snored as she walked by their rooms. Once in her bedroom, she turned up the lamp and kicked off her shoes. She had just enough space in her room for a bed and short dresser. She closed and locked the window and settled onto the bed to read.

Sacramento seemed to still be growing. The city had so many stores to choose from and several seemed to be hiring. She read every advertisement. Considering her current experience, working in a hotel might be possible. She turned to the last page and found an advertisement for a family run restaurant. Something about working with a family spoke to her and she folded up the paper to where the place's address showed.

Fiona folded up the paper and turned down the lamp. Used to undressing in the darkened room, she quickly changed into a nightgown. She retrieved her mother's writing lap desk and settled in under the covers. After reaching over and turning up the lamp again, she began to compose her letter requesting a job at the restaurant.

Finished, she set the letter on the dresser. She'd tell Mason about her plans as soon as possible. Rob still irritated her, and she couldn't talk to John or she'd cry. Randall was her friend and she felt bad about quitting work at the Carson City station without telling him her reasons. She didn't want him to worry so she pulled out a fresh sheet of paper to write a letter to him.

A smart woman might let her heart fall for a man like Randall. He was everything a good man should be. Fiona sighed and begin writing down her reasons for leaving. One by one, she listed finer living conditions, gaining a chance to talk with other women, and easier access to the markets. She reread everything she'd written and saw no need to mention anything about John's betrayal by gambling for her.

Fiona signed her name and reached to lay that letter next to the first. She put away her writing desk before turning down the lamp. Already under the covers, she nestled in and closed her eyes. The letters could go out as early as tomorrow noon. Only, sending anything via ordinary stage mail would take a week at least to get an answer.

She opened her eyes. If she waited too long, the position might be filled by the time she could send a reply. Even then, what if they said no? There'd be another letter, another wait, and all for another refusal. She turned over onto her other side. With the money she had saved, going on to Sacramento, staying in town, and searching from there would give her the fastest results. She'd just have to apply in person.

Now completely awake, Fiona knew she'd have to tell Mason about her plans. She threw off the covers and crept out of her room to where he usually slept. No one was there. She glanced around, listening for his voice in the quiet. A few men talked on the front porch. She'd much rather search for him there than accidently run into John in one of the bedrooms.

She crept into the parlor and froze when a floorboard squeaked behind her.

Mason hissed, "What in God's Creation are you

doing out here in your bedclothes?"

"Would you believe looking for you?"

He frowned. "I'd like to."

"Come on, let's talk in my room." She led him down the hall and went to sit on her bed.

He followed her inside, closed the door, and said, "What's so important you need to wander around half naked?"

Ignoring her irritation over his choice of words, she patted the blanket beside her. "We need to talk."

"All right." Mason went to sit beside her. The wooden frame squeaked as he said, "He came to me and asked about you. I didn't know what you'd said, so I told him to wait until tomorrow and you'd cooled off a little."

She frowned, not knowing how to feel; happy because she wouldn't have to tell Mason a long story about what happened, or angry because he'd heard it from someone else. And, she could guess which turkey was doing the squawking. "He? Do you mean John?"

Mason shrugged. "Who else has been moping around like a lost puppy?"

So they had talked. Despite her anger over his actions, she had to admire John's determination. "Never mind him. I care for him, but he's a gambler who won't be able to change his ways."

A few seconds passed before he finally said, "I don't know, Fee. He seemed very certain he could."

A thin crack began in her wall of resisting John. She wanted to believe he could change for her. Give up his gambling ways and be a partner in life and love, eventually. A small voice inside her added, just like she'd wanted to believe their father when he said never again. She sighed, tears beginning to fill her eyes. "So did Da. Every time."

"True." Mason put his arm around her. "So? I assume you're wanting to say more than John's in your past."

"I do. I've made a decision." She rested her head on his shoulder. "You won't like this, but I've decided to take another job in Sacramento."

He was silent for a moment. "Where?"

She hadn't sent the letter to the family restaurant and didn't want to jinx anything by saying her hopes out loud. "I don't know, exactly."

"You've thought this through?"

She nodded. All of her plans were for the best, really. "Completely."

"Will leaving make you happy?"

"Eventually, yes," she replied as if she believed her own words.

"Then you have my blessing, but I can't leave my best sister alone in a big city. I'll stay on here to save a little more money before I move to wherever you are."

Relief from not being by herself flooded her as did a little bit of guilt over Mason changing his plans for her. She rested her head against his shoulder. "All right, but will following me make you happy?"

He chuckled. "Eventually." After a few seconds, he asked, "Have you told Bill you're leaving?"

"No one else knows but you."

"What if he wants you to stay here and work? Offers you more money?"

Fiona hadn't considered Bill doing such a thing. But what if he did? Could she stay and see John every day and resist him? "I can't and I won't."

"Not even if he brought in an ice box for your food?"

She smiled, imagining having a station refrigerator to freely use. It'd be heavenly for sure. "I'd be tempted, yes, but no. My life is somewhere else."

CHAPTER ELEVEN

Fiona smiled and placed the food in front of her customer. If they were home in Ireland, she'd curtsey and call him m'lord. No one did such a thing here in the States. Yet the urge to give into a lifetime of manners tempted her. "Let me know if you require anything else, sir."

"Certainly, young lady."

She went back to the kitchen while making a note to check his water in a few minutes.

The family run restaurant she'd applied to when she'd first gotten to Sacramento hired her immediately. She'd been working for the Doyles a week and already applauded her decision to leave Carson City.

Except she wondered if....

No. Here was her new life and she loved it. The good, honest people running the business said she fit their needs, and she'd found a charming little apartment a few blocks from where she worked. Sacramento was a thriving community. She'd even found a nice church to attend. Her life was better than she'd ever dreamed back home.

She grabbed a water pitcher and circled the room. The service bell rang, telling her a table's order was finished. She smiled at a young family and hurried to the kitchen. Barney Doyle stood behind the large stove with a spatula. She picked up the plates while saying, "Looks like the lunch rush is nearly over."

"Good, because I'm about out of eggs." The beefy man began scraping the grill top. "Go on but come back after."

"Will do." She hurried out with the food, placing the meals in front of the customers. Satisfied everyone was happy, she glanced once more around the room to check the few customers still there. No one motioned to her so she hurried back to the kitchen. "Did you need something done?"

"Yes, a run to the market for me before dinner. I'd send Frank but he's cried off, saying he had plans or something." He wiped his hands on a towel which had seen better days. "Mrs. Doyle's with Larry and can't. There's a list on the counter for what we need and be sure to add anything you might want, too, my treat for going on such short notice."

"What?" She took the paper and shoved it in her skirt pocket. "You can't be paying me wages and picking up my grocery tab. You have a business to think of."

He pointed at her with a grin. "Now see here. If I want to treat my best employee well, that's my business and not yours."

"Your only employee, and it won't be your business for long with your spending on me."

He laughed. "Fine then. If it'll make you happy, only get half of what you need. And tell Frank to stop reading long enough to close up."

"We're lucky he looks up long enough to ring up the bills," she quipped.

"I agree. Maybe when I retire, Larry will be my successor around here while Frank's out curing the world."

"Probably so." Fiona returned his smile. She went out to tell the oldest son, Frank, about closing up and check on her last few customers. When she entered the main dining room, a lanky cowboy resembling John gave her a start.

Every halfway handsome young man resembling him had had the same effect on her. Irritated with her surge of happiness at the thought of him coming here for her, she snorted in disgust. Her mind knew better than her traitorous heart. She renewed her vow to have no time for gambling fools like him.

She went over to the Doyle's oldest son. "Frank, your father wants you to close up."

He didn't look up from his book of the day. "All right. After this page."

"Be sure to or he'll be unhappy," she said and he grunted. A couple days of working there and she figured out he'd need a push or "one more page" turned into the whole book. "I'll remind you before I leave for the market."

"He's sending you?" he asked. When she nodded, he grinned. "Mind picking up the daily paper? I'll tell Pa it's for me."

"Fine, as long as you share," Fiona countered.

"It's a deal."

She returned his smile and stepped back as her customer stepped up to pay. After dealing with pony boys for the past several months, the man seemed very refined. His clothes were clean and pressed. Nothing marred the black of his jacket or pants, and his shirt was the crispest starched white cotton she'd ever seen. She could imagine him as a banker or anything else financial. He gave her a nod. "Excellent meal, miss."

"Thank you. I'll be sure to tell the cook." She went and turned the sign to closed. As soon as the man left, she turned to Frank. "Lock up after me, please?"

He sighed and put down his book. "Go ahead."

She waited until he came out from behind the sales counter before leaving the building. Mason had been the same way at thirteen, all wrapped up in his own head. She'd been the one to drag him out of his daydreams every so often, he needed to remember there was a world out there. Thank goodness he'd learned his lesson as an adult. The youngest Doyle, Larry, was a baby toddling around. While she liked him just fine, Fiona would rather have her own business by the time he was old enough to help out in the restaurant.

Being entrusted with the Doyles' credit was a responsibility Fiona didn't take lightly. The last time she'd been shopping, all of the store owners knew who Barney was and greeted her with a smile. She checked the list while several horses and buggies rolled by. They needed several cuts of meat for the rest of the week, and milk, eggs, flour, lard, and vegetables. Her first stop would be the butcher across the street.

She paused at the butcher's doorway. Who knew a person could miss a garden, but there you go. She did miss her plants. All she could hope for was whoever took her place at the Express station kept the plot weeded. Refocusing on her shopping, she pushed the door open and first noticed the cold air and the mouthwatering smell of spices. A portly middle-aged man stood behind a counter working.

"Hello, miss. What can we do for you?"

He had a gravelly voice with an accent she couldn't quite place. Fiona smiled at him. "I'm here for Doyle's Restaurant." She glanced at her list. "He says he wants his usual." She frowned and admitted, "I'm not sure I know what he means."

"You're his new girl, aren't you?" the lanky man behind the display case shook his head when she nodded. "He can't keep employees and I told him, you gotta start hiring the older or married women. These young pretty ones, you can't keep them. They're always running off to get married with some starry-eyed man panning for gold or working for the Pony Express."

Fiona smiled at him mentioning a topic she knew very well. "None of the Express riders are married. A few might be, but most live a very solitary life with no family to speak of."

He grinned, too, and rested his beefy arms on top of the display case. "Sounds like the voice of experience to me. Is there a fella you know who's lonely for you? 'Cause I'll bet Doyle will have to hire another pretty girl to bring in the customers before too long."

Her face heated and shook her head. "No, not anymore, and I don't plan on Mr. Doyle needing someone to replace me. I know about the Express because my brother is a rider."

The butcher went back to preparing the meat order for the restaurant. "Ah, well. Don't mind me, then.

What I know of their life is what I read in the newspaper." He pulled out a length of paper and began packaging the meat into neat bundles. "Tell you what. Doyle's order is a lot for anyone to carry while shopping. I can have this delivered later this afternoon, no extra charge."

The bundle did seem a bit unwieldy and the butcher was only her first stop. She nodded and put the list back in her pocket. "If you don't mind and there's no charge, then yes. I'd really appreciate your doing so."

He pushed the wrapped package to her over the case. "Great. I'll send someone around in an hour or so, and he's been there before. He's also a handsome young fella so if you hurry back to Doyle's, you might catch him when he comes by with the delivery."

She laughed and turned toward the door. "Thank you for thinking of me and I'll try to meet him if possible." Another customer came in, so she left with a small wave. Once outside, she sighed. The butcher seemed like a nice enough guy despite being a little more familiar than she was used anyone being.

She walked along, people watching and window shopping along the way. To her dismay, every man reminding her of John turned her head or gained a second look from her. She sighed and focused on the next store. All she'd need was plenty of time to stop caring so much for him.

The general grocer was closest and several items from the list were there. She stopped a newsboy and bought a paper from him. None of the next storeowners were as friendly as the butcher. Still, they were kind and seemed to think highly of Mr. Doyle. Fiona hurried back to the restaurant. Not so much to meet the deliveryman but more due to the newspaper in her hands.

She went in through the back door, meeting a deliveryman on his way out. Yes, he was handsome, but he wasn't John. Mr. Doyle was busy putting away the meat order so she chose a distance far enough away to give him room to work. "The grocery had fresh apricots so I bought up a few for a pie."

He came over and picked one up. "Excellent! I'll use them this evening, if we're slow enough."

"Let me know if you need help," she said over her shoulder. "Frank and I will be cleaning and then reading the newspaper."

"Will do. Don't let him make excuses for not helping you."

"Yes, sir," she replied and went on to find the younger Doyle at the cash register. "Here's something new for us to read."

"I heard. Pa is still going on about us cleaning up around here."

She wanted to make the work fun or at least bearable enough for Frank to lose his bad attitude. "So? I'll read a page while you clean, then we swap places for a page. Whoever finishes cleaning first wins a prize your father picks."

Frank narrowed his eyes. "You won't keep reading until I'm done and let me win?"

"Like you did to me yesterday?" She tried not to smile at his shamefaced expression from being caught at trying to trick her. "No. One page only. Like musical chairs, only with reading."

"Very well. I'll wipe down tables." He went toward the back. "One page only!"

She chuckled and said so he'd hear, "One, I promise." She sat on the stool he usually occupied and scanned the front page. Discussions of slavery, Indian attacks, the new President all dominated the paper. A headline concerning the Pony Express caught her eye and she began reading.

Fiona stared at the text, the letters blurring. All of the words made perfect sense, yet she couldn't understand. Natives attacked and burned Cold Springs Station to the ground. No survivors. The station had been John's usual place to stay before coming back to Carson City. And if Mason had been there during the raid, too? Both men could already be dead and buried.

She sobbed while trying to not imagine their graves. Mason had to be all right, and John? She wiped the tears rolling down her cheeks. A part of her had wanted him to come to Sacramento after her, declaring his love and promising to never gamble again. She turned her back to the register so no one would see her cry. John had already done everything she wanted, yet she'd turned him down and came here. He'd been the man she asked him to be and now he could be dead somewhere along with her brother.

Fiona pressed the back of a trembling hand to her forehead and tried to be calm. Before going to bed that evening, she needed to write to Bill and ensure both men were safe.

CHAPTER TWELVE

John stared up at the sign. This had to be where Fiona was. He peeked into the restaurant but couldn't tell if she was in there. If he didn't say every word correctly, he'd lose her for good. He put his sweaty hands into his pockets and took a deep breath before slowly exhaling. This one chance had to count.

He pushed open the door and stepped inside. A teenaged boy sat at a cash register with a book in his hand. "Hello."

The youngster glanced up. "Nice shiner."

"Thank you. I earned it."

"I reckon." He shrugged and said in a well-rehearsed monotone, "Welcome to Doyle's. Have a seat and our server will be with you in a moment."

Feeling a bit dismissed, John found a seat at a table near the back. He intended to make throwing him out as difficult as possible for her, he'd need every moment to convince her to give him a second chance. He might be wasting his time by being here but he had to try. Nothing in his world was good without her.

He looked at everything, the place seemed clean and welcoming.

Fiona walked out of the back kitchen loaded down with full plates. She walked past him as if he wasn't there. He watched as she worked, chatting with the group of people. It had only been a week, nearly two, since he'd last seen her. Everything had changed, yet she looked the same as ever. She turned toward him and the kitchen, stopping cold when their eyes met. A flash of happiness crossed her face before she frowned. His elation turned to dust when she walked up to him with her hands on her hips.

"So. Mason told you where I was? How is he?"

"He did tell me and he's fine." Her eyes were a little red rimmed as if she'd been crying recently. He clasped his hands together to keep from reaching out and hugging her.

"Hmph." She glared at him. "I'm glad you both weren't killed in the Cold Springs attack. I'd only read what happened there this afternoon."

Her anger hurt. He kept his focus on her and tried to keep the emotion from his voice. "I was at Sand Springs and Mason was at Fort Churchill that day. Rob had ridden on to Fish Creek while Hyatt, Burt, and Jim didn't make it out before the place burned to the ground."

Her eyes watered and she stared down at the ground. "I'm so sorry for your loss."

John had to clear his throat before saying, "So am I. They were good men and hard workers. Troops have been sent to find the attackers."

"Not that there needs to be more bloodshed, but I'm glad the deed won't go unpunished." She glanced up at him. "I need to check on the customers. Wait here and think about telling me why you have a black eye."

Fiona wanted him to stay? Hope rose in him and he tried to not be so optimistic but failed. He managed to keep from doing anything more than calmly respond to her. "I'll do anything as long as you come back."

She gave him a slight frown and hurried off. He watched as she refilled glasses, served food, and cleared away plates. She disappeared into the kitchen and soon after, a huge brawny man wearing a crude apron came out and walked up to him. "You're here to see Fiona?"

John stood and still had to look up to the man. "I am."

He crossed arms, thick as young tree trunks. "Are you the reason she's here and not in Carson City?"

"Afraid so." John lifted his chin. "I came here to talk her into going home with me."

The man scowled at John for a few moments before his expression relaxed. He put his hands on his hips and shook his head. "Aw hell. I'm gonna lose another good employee."

"No, you won't," Fiona said as she walked up to both men. "I have no plans to go anywhere."

The man looked from Fiona to John and back again. "We'll see." He smiled at her. "I can give you fifteen minutes but that's all until closing."

"Fine," she said. "That's more than long enough to send him on his way."

Her boss grinned and headed for the kitchen. "Don't be so hasty. He's free to stay and order as much as he'd like."

She frowned before saying, "All right, we won't be long." Turning to John, she made a "follow me" motion. "Come on out back. We'll not be disturbing the customers out there."

He stood and did as she'd said, following her through the kitchen and storeroom, before stepping outside. The alley wasn't as busy as the road out front, but there were people milling around, throwing out dirty water, and stacking trash along the walls. He'd prefer any other place, but this might be his last opportunity to convince her of anything. "You'd asked about my black eye. It's thanks to my own stupidity. Mason asked if I'd gambled for you before knowing about your father and I was honest. I said I knew your history but had to win you for myself and he decked me."

She reached over and pulled away a lock of his hair from his eyebrow. "He didn't mess around, that's for sure. It's already trying to turn a darker purple. Going by the black eyes he's had, I'd guess yours will be here for a week or two more."

John leaned into her touch as if it were a caress instead of an impartial examination. "Hitting me must have made him feel better or worse because soon after, he told me where you'd gone to."

Fiona let his hair fall back into place with a slight smile. "He could never keep a secret."

"I'm glad he didn't." John looked down at the ground for mud before kneeling on one knee. "We don't have very long to talk before you need to go back inside."

"John, I don't think—" she began.

"Shh. I need to tell you something important and hear me out, all right?" he said and when she nodded, he took both of her hands in his. "Marry me. I know you love me. You know what my plans were, but everything changed when I met you."

She shook her head. "You had no plans."

"I didn't. Not until I realized the kind of strong, beautiful, and loving woman you are. I fell in love with you so fast, it scared me and upset all the plans I thought I hadn't made." Her slight grin gave him hope. He returned her smile and said, "Marry me. Be my wife and make my heart whole again."

She pulled her hands from his. "No, John, I can't. I won't."

His entire body felt cracked in two but he couldn't let her go so easily. He stood up and put a hand over his heart. "You're scared to trust me. I understand why, but I vow to never gamble again. Not even if you refuse to marry me, I'll never bet on anything."

"I've heard that promise before."

"You have, but not from me. I don't break my promises." He shook his head. "I don't know what to do, what to say, that's enough for you to believe me. All I can do is live every minute showing you how I feel. Creating a home and life together where we're both happy and in love. I never thought I was ready until I kissed you."

"You gambled for me, John. You knew what had happened with my Da and his gaming yet you did it anyway."

"I did. It took losing the hand to realize I was playing for keeps." He caressed her face. "I can promise no more gambling, but can't promise I'll stop loving you."

"Suppose a woman did believe you'd stop betting on courting her. Suppose she admitted to loving you.

Would you miss being with your friends, drinking and playing cards? A woman who loved you might not want your feeling resentful toward her."

Her words warmed him like a winter sun peeking over high mountains, melting the frost. He wanted to take her in his arms and swing her around but kept still. She wasn't firmly convinced just yet or she'd be hugging him first. He smiled and stared into her eyes. "I don't need to play games ever again because I've just won the biggest prize in the world."

"Oh? What is this grand prize, then?"

His response sounded florid in his mind before he said the words, but was honest. "Your love is the only reward I want."

"I see," Fiona said while crossing her arms. She examined him up and down before adding, "So." She bumped the side of her hip against his. "Where do you plan on spending the night, pony boy?"

"I hadn't thought that far ahead," he said before catching the playful glint in her eyes. He shrugged as casually as he could. "I guess in a stable or on a blanket outside of town. Somewhere cold, lonely, and not cozied up to you."

She laughed. "It's nearly summer, boyo. Try harder to gain an offer to stay with me. You'll not be getting into my bedroom if you give up this easily."

He struggled to keep calm while asking, "I'll have to work for it?"

Her eyes narrowed. "Something like that, yes."

The way she was looking at him with a shy and almost trusting face? He could move mountains and drain oceans for her. Whatever she wanted or needed, and he'd do anything to make sure she was happy with him. He caressed her cheek and quietly said, "I'm game."

Fiona put her hands on his chest as if to push him away. "John…"

"Fine. I fold." He pulled her into his arms and kissed her nose. "Will you stop all this resisting how you feel and marry me so I can take you to my bedroom as often as want?"

She leaned back and tilted her head. "That's not much of a deal for me."

"You greedy little cuss," he teased and had no doubt she'd succeed in any business she decided to run. "All right. How about this deal? I give you all of my love, devotion, and the rest of my life to live with you. Will all of that, plus my bedroom, convince you?"

She gave him a long, lingering kiss before saying, "Yes, and I'll give every bit of the same to you. Is it a deal?"

John grinned but couldn't keep his gaze from Fiona's. "You bet."

ABOUT THE AUTHOR

With an overactive imagination and a love for writing, Laura Stapleton decided to type out her daydreams and what if's. She currently lives in Kansas City with her husband and a few cats. When not at the computer, you'll find her in the park for a jog or at the yarn store's clearance section.

If you enjoyed this story, please consider leaving me a review. I'd love to learn more about my readers so if you prefer, you can contact me via the links below. I always welcome constructive advice and hoped you liked reading this story.

Find me online at https://twitter.com/LauraLStapleton, www.facebook.com/LLStapleton and at http://lauralstapleton.com. Subscribe to my newsletter to keep up on the latest and join my Facebook group at Laura's Favorite Readers.

69652639R00070

Made in the USA
Middletown, DE
21 September 2019